ARMAGEDDON COMETH

SPECIES INTERVENTION

#6609

J.K. Accinni

E.K. Publishing
Bradenton, FL(s/b Lakewood Ranch)

This is a work of fiction. Names, characters, places and incidents either are the product of the author's imagination or are used fictitiously and any resemblance to actual persons, living or dead, business establishments, events, or locales is entirely coincidental.

ARMAGEDDON COMETH
SPECIES INTERVENTION #6609
J.K. Accinni

ISBN: 978-0-9899769-2-3

An E. K. Publishing book published in arrangement with the author, Bradenton (s/b Lakewood Ranch), FL.

Copyright © 2012 J.K. Accinni
Editing by LionheART Publishing House

Other Books by J.K. Accinni:

Baby (Species Intervention #6609, Book 1)

Echo (Species Intervention #6609, Book 2)

Armageddon Cometh (Species Intervention #6609, Book 3)

Hive (Species Intervention #6609 Book 4)

Evil Among Us (Species Intervention #6609, Book 5)

The One (Species Intervention #6609, Book 6)

Alien Species Intervention Books 1-3

Dedication

I would like to thank my mom, Jane, for her unflagging support. She never once thought to even question my capabilities. I owe so much to my one true love, Wil, whose honest clear sweetness and support gave me something to live up to.

I would like to thank the phenomenally talented artists who granted me the rights to their work for my covers: Adam Taylor, United Kingdom, England—*Baby;* Jonas Jedicke, Berlin, Germany—*Armageddon Cometh* and *The One;* Terry Rogers, Gainesville, Florida—*Hive.*

And lastly, I want to acknowledge my four-legged children: Barney, Toby, Molly, Teddy and Echo, and all of my children who are waiting for me over the Rainbow Bridge. They are what bring all the richness and laughter into my life.

Chapter 1
2056 AD

The pounding on Scotty's door came late in the morning.

"Scotty, get out here right now. *Scotty!*"

"Alright, alright." Going to the door, he found Abby and Jose glaring at him.

"What the *hell* did you do?" Jose stood with his hands on his hips, rocking back on his heels, his face purple. Abby's hands held him back, but she didn't look much happier.

"What's the fuss? Hey, can you let the dogs out? I'll be down in a few minutes." He rubbed his eyes, half asleep.

"I'm not kidding, Scotty. You've got five minutes." They turned on their heels, chasing the dogs down the staircase.

Scotty hurried down the stairs, rubbing his sleepy eyes and yawning. Stealing a quick peek out the terrace doors, he could feel the day was a roaster in the making. He glanced around for Echo, seeing Abby and Jose at the kitchen table, scouring the newspaper. Jose picked up the front page, smacking it down in Scotty's direction with such force it fell to the floor. Picking it up, he scanned the headline.

Oh, boy. How in the world did it hit the paper so fast? They must have bumped another story. Scanning the facts, the paper reported the dogs they saved had been taken to the local shelter. Dognapping victims were being advised to stop by to examine the dogs. Human bones taken to coroner; weapons in abandoned vehicles; fighting apparatus; unexplained crime scene; copious amounts of animal blood; authorities stumped etc., etc. . .

Yeah, Scotty thought as he put the paper down. *They know all the facts except who did it and why.* Not surprised, he felt no guilt. No

1

way could either he or Echo have allowed the dogfighting to continue. It was a way of life with those ignorant hillbilly assholes. They didn't change. No second chances for them. They hadn't given the dogs any second chances. No, all they'd received was skulls bashed in with a baseball bat or sledge hammer, or being chewed to death as prey for the fighting dogs.

Tears came to his eyes as he thought about the innocence of the tragic pets stolen from their suburban lawns and loving homes, with no understanding of why they had been torn away. The kind of man who could do this to an animal was on par with a pedophile. They both preyed on the innocent for their own gratification and disposed of the evidence through merciless torture and murder. They were both predators, their predilection hardwired into their brains. The only difference was that pedophiles *knew* what they did was wrong. The other bastards thought they had a God-given right. Well, where the hell was God when the agony and suffering went down? The scum in the woods sure wouldn't be touching another helpless dog again and he *was not sorry*.

"Where were you last night?" Jose looked steamed. Glancing at Abby for help, he knew he was on his own, her face reflected only worry.

"There's no sense denying it, Scotty, the skeletons tell the story. You can't just go around killing people. Was Echo with you?" Turning to Abby, Scotty hung his head. He felt an aura caress his mind as Echo spoke up. "Brother Scotty did not kill anyone."

Jose stood up, disappointment on his face. "Echo, please don't tell me it was you."

"It was not me, Brother Jose. But they *needed* to die. They were very evil."

"Then who was it? How did they die?" Jose sat down, his posture seething with disbelief.

"It was the Womb."

"You saw the Womb? Come on, cut the crap."

"I did, Jose. I saw it."

Jose took a deep breath, a grenade ready to explode. His fingers drummed impatiently on the table, the tempo escalating. "I can't deal with this right now. Can you please keep an eye on him? I'm not in the mood for fairy tales." Jose abruptly rose up from the table and stalked out of the room. Scotty scratched his head, ready to condemn Jose's overreaction.

"What's with him?"

"I don't know, just stress. Promise me you'll stay around the house? Stay out of trouble?"

"Yeah, I'm going back to bed if you don't mind. I have plans later with Echo and the dogs, if that's okay?" Scotty sounded contrite, looking to placate Abby. Why blow up on her anyway? He knew he could always count on his sister to be in his corner first and ask questions later.

"Don't leave the island." She put her hand on his. "You know we have to talk about this sometime."

"Yeah, just later. Please, Ab."

She patted his hand again. "Okay, go back to bed, kiddo." Abby smiled, getting up to give him a quick hug. "I understand. I know how much creatures mean to you. Don't take what Jose says to heart. He's just trying to keep us on the down low and out of the public eye. I'll calm him down. He just isn't as nutty crazy as you are about creatures, so he doesn't get it."

"Don't worry, Ab, I'll convert him, sooner or later." As Scotty left the room to head up the stairs, the entire posse, including Echo, trundled up the stairs behind him, back to bed.

Chapter 2

Scotty slept late into the afternoon, Echo and Barney already outside. Throwing on a pair of denim cutoffs and a terry cloth shirt, he ran down the grand staircase out to the terrace, hunting for his posse.

Putting the memory of last night behind him for now, he allowed himself to get jazzed about the surprise he had planned for Echo. This was just for her. Whistling for the gang, they came running in a pack; Echo holding on tight to Barney as Penny and Mimi brought up the rear. Appearing at the front of the house, Scotty cautiously slipped Echo inside the garage, mindful of unwelcome eyes.

As everyone piled into his Jeep, he lifted a baby carriage into the back of the truck, smoothing down the opaque netting which hung down over the opening. Looking up as he closed the Jeep door, Kane shouted to him from the mouth of the garage, his muscled arms standing out in relief, the sun glazing the sweat beaded on his skin.

"What's you up to, Scotty?" His big sleepy brown eyes squinted into the cool shade of the garage.

"What are you doing here, Kane? Shouldn't you be down at the dock with your father?" Scotty was annoyed, Kane was always trying to suck up or butt in. Penny slipped out of the vehicle and pranced over to Kane where he squatted, rubbing the soft clean fur on her well-formed head.

"Na, he's having a meeting with Jose, so I have a few hours off. Thought I'd offer my services if you wanted to take your little put-put out." Kane smiled innocently.

"I think I'll pass . . . thanks anyway. Penny, let's go, girl." Hearing Penny whine, he saw Kane had taken a hard, fast grip on her. Sizing up the situation, he remembered Kane weighed about fifty pounds more than him, all solid muscle. Uneasy, he tried for a light tone.

"You mind letting go of my dog?"

"Why don't you come get her? Or are you afraid to get your pretty-boy golden curls mussed up?" Kane tensed his muscles, a hard light in his eyes. Knowing a fight was inevitable, Scotty came out from behind the vehicle, noting Echo climbing down from her seat. *Oh, no.*

Before anyone could make another move, Barney bounded out of the vehicle, ran to Penny and lunged at Kane. Caught off guard, he fell flat onto his butt, sprawling on the driveway. Penny and Barney danced back to the vehicle, jumping in as Echo climbed back up to her seat where they all settled down.

With a laugh, Scotty got behind the wheel and started the Jeep. Feeling relieved, he edged out of the garage, giving a jaunty salute to Kane's enraged face, then headed down the road. *He'll calm down soon enough*, Scotty thought, trying to reassure himself. *Too bad he's such an ass.* His life left no time or room for a boat bum like Kane. They shared nothing in common.

Putting Kane out of his mind, he looked forward to the rest of the day. Several weeks ago, Scotty, Echo and Barney had by chance discovered a path from the main road around the island to the water. They had seen a tiny strip of sand that wound unimpeded down a stretch of beach. It begged them to explore. But how to do it without outing Echo in public? Simple solution: *a baby carriage.* Not an ordinary carriage, of course. Forced to take Peter into his confidence in order to obtain the carriage, he had altered the wheels for the beach. They needed to be wider to ride above the sand instead of sinking in. So Peter, the professional that he was, obtained just what he required without asking intrusive questions. What harm could he come to with a baby carriage, anyway?

The unyielding midday sun enshrouded them with its relentless swelter. Scotty slipped on his sunglasses, removed the doctored carriage from the Jeep, and placed a jug of water for the dogs in the storage compartment. Lifting the opaque netting, he boosted Echo into the carriage, pinning the netting to the top so Echo could see out.

"What do you think, girl? Do you like it? It's all yours."

"Is this an automobile, Brother Scotty? An automobile for *me*?" The aura in Scotty's mind swirled with golden fractals, almost blinding him.

"Yes, it's a very old style car, with no engine. It must be pushed and I'm happy to do it. Now we can play on the beach, as long as we're alone." Echo ran her fragile leather hands over the inside lining of the carriage.

"And what is the name of this automobile? Is it Jeep like yours?"

"Nope, a different manufacturer. It's called a Carriage. Modified. Just for you."

"Just for me . . ." The mind aura did not ask a question, it sounded more like a statement of wonder. "I need you in my heart, Brother Scotty." Echo reached out to Scotty. He picked her up, swinging her around in his arms as the dogs danced at his heels.

"Don't worry, Echo, I need you in my heart too." Laughing, he deposited her back in the carriage. Mimi stood on her hind legs, straining to see inside.

"You don't want to miss a thing, do you girl?" Lifting Mimi, Scotty deposited her in the carriage with Echo.

"Brother Scotty, I want My Barney to ride too."

"No, Echo, that boy's just too big. Mimi is perfect. She's too little for the sand and she's your camouflage in case someone comes poking around. You just remember to dive under the covers and pull down the netting. No one will be the wiser."

The whole gang headed for the sand, Scotty pushing the carriage over the scrub weeds until they reached the tiny beach. They were alone except for the closest mansion about five hundred feet away. They were within distant eyeshot of the mansion's deep-water dock, containing two yachts, one a monster for sure. Scotty doubted anyone glancing their way would be able to tell what kind of dogs played on the beach, let alone how many. If approached, he would scoop up Echo and deposit her in the carriage. Little Mimi would languish there, ostensibly recovering from an injury. The ruse gave all of them a small, precious sense of freedom.

Penny loved jumping in the air after the gulls, never getting close, but convinced she was keeping them all safe from the noisy wheeling birds. Mimi watched, glassy eyed and complacent, from the carriage as Echo and Scotty chased Barney around the edge of the water, jumping and playing games of doggy tag. Echo loved being *it*, riding on Barney's back as they chased down Penny and Scotty. Scotty kept his eye on them all, laughing at their antics or tossing a blue rubber ball for them to scramble after.

From out of nowhere, a high-pitched scream came from the direction of the mansion with the yachts, followed by the sight of a miniature chocolate furry bullet streaming toward them on the beach. The bullet was being chased by a young girl yelling frantically for it to stop. How a tiny ball of curly brown fur could keep up that pace in the hot sun was unbelievable. It danced like a ping pong ball, bouncing from one dog to another to Scotty to Echo, where it stopped, panting and staring, its dinky brown paws flush on the sand, its body prone like a sphinx. Scotty scooped up Echo, deposited her in the carriage with Mimi, then grabbed the water canister as the furry bullet's pretty mistress flopped down on the sand next to it.

Scotty poured some water for their furry guest. He sat on the sand, joined by Barney and Penny.

"Thanks for the water, Ted gets carried away sometimes. He loves to show off for people. I'm Chloe. You a dog sitter? They can't possibly all be yours."

"Yeah, they're all mine. What kind of shrimpy mutt is Ted?"

"He's a Shih Tzu/teacup poodle. He's six pounds with a one-hundred-pound personality. Pure alpha. Teddy, come here." Chloe hung her head, shaking it sorrowfully as she watched Teddy climb up Penny's back as she lay in the sand. He was so tiny, fifty-five pound

Penny seemed unaware that he was there as he made his way up to her ear, which he straddled and proceeded to mate with.

"I'm Scotty Preston," he said, watching the spectacle in front of him. "We live over on Mango Lane. You live there?" Pointing to the mansion with the deep-water dock, Scotty saw her nod.

"What's in the carriage? You got a kid here?" Getting up, Chloe turned to the carriage. Scotty beat her to it, adjusting the netting.

"No, that's just Mimi, she's a Shih Tzu too, a puppy mill rescue. She can't walk right now. She's recovering from a spinal operation. This helps me get her outside so she can be with us."

Chloe looked in. "Let me see. Oh, she looks like a little skunk. That's so sweet of you."

Scotty grabbed the handle of the carriage and prepared to run. Chloe sat back down on the sand. He relaxed and joined her, appraising her athletic build.

"You must be hot. Isn't that terry cloth? It's okay if you want to take off your shirt."

"No, I'm good."

Chloe and Scotty talked for another hour or so. Scotty felt comfortable with her, common ground easy to find. He sensed a loneliness in her which felt familiar. She was the first teenager other than Kane who he had spoken to in almost a year.

Even though at fifteen she was two years younger than him—although she had mentioned she had a birthday coming up soon—he felt comfortable enough to swap cell numbers, noticing she sure wasn't hard to look at. He wished he could be smoother with the ladies, but he needed a lot of practice before he could set his childhood complexes aside.

"Maybe you can come visit me at my house. We have monkeys, what do you think of that? They don't belong to me, they belong to my uncle. He looks after me when my dad's away. My mom's dead," she said, wiping an unexpected stray tear. I'm sorry, I didn't mean—"

"No, Chloe, I get it. It's okay. My mom died too, about a year ago. My sister and I still aren't normal yet either. That'd be cool if I could see your uncle's monkeys," he said, changing the subject.

Chloe turned away, shading her eyes as she stared past Scotty down the beach. Barney struggled to his feet, running off in the same direction.

"We've got company. Your dog seems happy to see him." Barney was doing his best to lick the hair off Jose's legs.

"That's my sister's boyfriend. He's my best friend too."

Jose reached the group, his eyes searching cautiously in acknowledgment of Scotty's company.

"Where's Echo?" Jose sounded worried. Chloe looked at the dogs.

"Did I miss one?"

"No, Echo's in the carriage with Mimi. She's just a cat we have," Scotty said quickly, jumping up and introducing them, pointing to Chloe's house down the beach.

"I think that little guy belongs to you, young lady?" Teddy was blissfully ignoring everyone, going to town on Penny's ear again.

Getting up out of the sand, Chloe laughed as she detached Teddy from the springer's ear, said goodbye, then headed down the beach to her house. She turned once, giving them all a wave. Jose knelt in the sand, removed his sunglasses and stroked Penny's coppery fur.

"Chloe seems like a nice girl. This the first time you met her?"

"Yeah, we just needed to get away from the house for a while. Don't worry, we were careful. Chloe invited me to her house. I'd like to go. She says her uncle lives there with a collection of monkeys. That'd be cool."

"Yeah, monkeys are cool. I knew a few when I was little, a long time ago." Jose's face took on a distant haunted look, his eyes unreadable. Scotty thought to ask him about it when, just as fast as they had clouded, his eyes cleared. Maybe he had imagined it. Jose's eyes now glowed so golden they were hard to read, anyway.

"Wouldn't mind seeing them myself. Just let me know when you leave the grounds next time." Going to the carriage, he lifted the netting. Two heads popped up.

"Hello, Brother Jose, Look at my new automobile." Echo's colorful aura swirled languidly.

"Your new automobile?"

"Yes, it is a Carriage, modified just for me. I am sorry I cannot give you a ride, but you have your own car. Mine is a gift from Brother Scotty."

"Yeah, real nice, Echo. That Scotty is just full of surprises. Okay, let's saddle up, guys. I need to have a word with Scotty, and you'd better get home now." As they walked back to their cars, Jose told Scotty about his impending trip to New Jersey.

"That's great," Scotty said, realizing Jose had decided to drop the issue of last night's rescue. He must be pretty occupied with the search for his family. They all missed Mama Diaz, being the only adult maternal presence left in their lives. And he missed Emma and Bonnie. They wouldn't care how funny he looked. If Jose located the rest of the family and they joined them in Sarasota, his life would be much more normal. Things were starting to look up. His thoughts drifted back to Chloe. *Yeah*, he smiled to himself, *things are definitely looking up.*

"Let's head back to the house. I'd like us to spend some time together with Abby before Peter takes me to the airport."

"Okay, I'll meet you back there." Jose walked off after making sure everyone was secure; Scotty followed in the baking afternoon sun.

Scotty sat at the kitchen table with Abby, trying to talk to her about meeting Chloe. Jose stood at the kitchen sink, listening to him chatter on. Abby sat in her ornamental pig-iron antique kitchen chair, oblivious to it all. She was staring at Echo who, for some unfathomable reason, sat plucking white hairs out of Barney's fur and holding them up to the sun. She guarded a small plastic jar sitting on the floor where she deposited the hairs. *Well*, thought Abby, *at least Echo's found something to occupy herself with.* Her attention turned moodily to Jose and Scotty, who were both staring at her.

"What?" They both started in on her at the same time.

"What are you guys yelling at me about? For Pete's sake." She lifted her heavy hair off her neck, radiating impatience and boredom. She stood up suddenly, her chair scraping noisily on the marble kitchen floor. The dogs startled out of their placid late-afternoon snooze, heads swiveling in unison to face Abby.

"Gee, doesn't anyone have anything to do except whine at me all the time?"

"Babe, we weren't whining at you at all, we were just—"

"Oh, so now I'm wrong about my own feelings?" She marched over to a cabinet, took down a glass and slammed it on the counter, inadvertently breaking it. Penny immediately got up to sniff the glass that had fallen on the floor.

"Watch out, Penny. Abby, the dogs are going to get hurt now." Scotty got up to clean the mess.

"So now I'm hurting the dogs? Really?"

Scotty started to open his mouth. Catching Jose's eye, he stayed silent.

"Come on, Ab." Jose moved to put his arms around her.

"Don't. I'm not in the mood." Shrugging him off, she pulled out another glass and let the cold water run, the sound calming her down. Filling her glass, she mumbled, "I'm sorry," then stalked out to the terrace where she remained for the rest of the evening, not even getting up to say goodbye to Jose as he left for the airport.

She hoped she could snap out of her malaise by the time Mama Diaz returned with the girls. Glancing down toward the dock, she saw Captain Cobby sitting alone, watching the sunset. She had been meaning to find the time to chat with him about the tension between

Kane and Scotty. Scotty had filled her in on the incident in the garage, and she hadn't liked the sound of what could have been a disaster if Scotty's secret had been exposed in the middle of a fight.

Slipping on her sunglasses, she adjusted her clothing, making sure everything remained properly concealed, then headed down to the dock.

Walking the short plank, she stuck her head in before going on deck.

"Permission to come aboard?"

Captain Cobby hurried to lend a hand, leaving his drink on the cocktail table near the captain's chair at the wheel.

"Ms. Abby, you know you don't ever need permission. The *Lucky Lady* belongs to you."

"I know, Captain, but I do like to observe the niceties where I can. I hope I'm not interrupting your evening."

"No, no, please join me." He led her over to the cocktail area where plush green and white striped outdoor chairs were strewn about. The area could hardly be called intimate as it appeared spacious enough to hold a reception for a hundred people.

Sitting down, she held up an empty Baccarat crystal glass, plucked off the outdoor sideboard. The captain hastened to fill it for her. She held the crystal, twirling it in the waning late afternoon sun, absently noting the similarity to Echo's antlers.

There had been a time when they had counted themselves lucky to have plastic glasses, and if colored all the better. The colored ones hid the scratches which collected on the cheap plastic. She shook her head imperceptibly as she waited for her wine to breathe, reflecting on the grandeur and glamour of the new life which had just been handed to them. Was she dreaming? Just the mere fact that she even *knew* red wine must breathe, startled her. Nothing about her new life felt real.

"Hope a Pinot Noir is okay."

Nodding, Abby took a sip, eyeing him over her glass. Captain

Cobby struck a rather handsome appearance, in an exciting, older, virile Italian kind of way. *It must be the thick, dark, curly hair,* she thought, forgetting that Jose used to have thick, dark, curly hair. They sat together, neither speaking, letting the lapping of gentle waves against the hull weave a calm and intimate ambience around them. Breaking their companionable silence, she asked, "Is Kane around tonight?"

"I'm disappointed. I hoped you were here to visit *me.*" Laughing, he gave her a quick wink.

"I *am* here to see you, Captain, I just didn't want our conversation overheard."

Leaning back in his chair, he nodded his head slowly, rubbing his strong weather-beaten hand across his closely cropped beard. He gently set down his wine glass, crossed his tanned arms and looked at her without a trace of humor.

"Is this about my son?"

Taken aback by his quick change of tone, Abby decided to tread softly. "Yes, Captain. I just hoped you and I can do something to bring the boys together, before any blood flies."

Relaxing a bit, the captain adopted a low confidential tone. "Kane has not had an easy go of it in life, Abby. His mother kept me from seeing him, then took off for God knows where. He lived with the notion I was dead. I did my best to find them, but my job on the water was not conducive to raising a child. I gave up pretty easily. When he turned ten, she suddenly showed up to dump the boy with me. You can imagine how it went from there. It's taken me a long time to get Kane to this point. He has a chip on his shoulder because he feels he wasn't wanted. He knows differently, now. But he'll always be that ten-year-old boy who was dumped with a stranger because his mother didn't want him anymore; a mother who betrayed him with a lie for ten years. We've not heard from her since."

Smiling gently, the captain looked deeply into her eyes. "Can I dare to ask you to cut him some slack and let the boys work it out themselves? I promise I'll guide him as much as I can without interfering."

Nodding, Abby stood up, extending her hands to clasp both of his. "I understand, Captain Cobby. I truly do. Scotty's upbringing was not that different from Kane's. Maybe if they each knew that, things would be easier for them. I'll leave the matter with you, after I have a talk with Scotty. Thank you for your time." With that, she released his hands, smiling as he tipped his glass to her in agreement.

Before leaving, Abby filled in a few details of Scotty's loveless relationship with his father and their parents' subsequent divorce. Comfortable with their understanding, Abby allowed the captain to give her a hand across the plank to the dock. With a grateful smile and wave, she walked back to the house, the moon guiding her path. She marveled at how everyone seemed to have a story of strife and pain. She wasn't the only one. Feeling refreshed, she began to look forward to Jose's return with Mama Diaz and the girls.

That night, Abby's restlessness fought against her desire to sleep. She opened her eyes, noticing it was past midnight. The moon made her uneasy, a quiet crescent gazing into her bedroom window like a peeping Tom hoping to catch her unaware. The shadows of the palm trees, backlit and morphing the yard into an eerie vista of lurking creatures, unnerved her.

Why couldn't she settle down? Her glance lingered on Jose's empty spot in the bed. She leaned over, breathing in the familiar musky smell of his fur, finding it reassuring. Rolling back to her side of the bed, she wrapped her hands around the cool cotton sheet, drawing it under her chin as she scrunched herself into a fetal position, her mind flashing a kaleidoscope of memories, hoping to latch onto a soothing one to lull her to sleep. Feeling her budding wings cramp underneath her, she gave up.

Rising, she shambled over to the windows, her sleeplessness leaving her feeling drugged and lethargic. Rubbing her temples and shaking out her wings, she flexed her tail. *Perhaps my sleeplessness has something to do with my mind's unconscious attempt to avoid reliving the recurring nightmare I've been having for weeks?* The memory of the nightmare sent shivers down her evolving backside, causing her tail to stir reflexively.

Without warning, she found herself reviewing the nightmare as she stood at the window fully awake. She observed herself standing in a deserted parking lot in front of an iron grill, bent and misshapen; the stanchions under which millions of children and adults passed in their quest to discover where the famous Bronx Zoo had once housed their favorite wild creatures. The stanchions no longer supported its proud sign. She scanned the soundless trees, denuded of life. They appeared as if they'd been flattened by a giant fist, pummeling them from the gray and wintry sky. She looked off to the blank horizon: the most famous skyline in the world—gone. Devastation. She felt the bitter cold seep through her golden fur, flakes of dirty brown snow slowly, soundlessly, covering her thick golden hair, even as she somehow knew it was the middle of summer.

She turned back to the ruined zoo, an irresistible compulsion. Without warning, she discovered herself floating over the crumbling exhibits on the zoo's decimated grounds. Formerly home to the many innocent creatures which had found themselves captive to man's misguided attempt to shape, control and destroy the lives of creatures he, in his hubris, thought belonged to him. The vacant exhibits all contained ominous piles of bleached bone ash. All that remained of some of the most exquisite, bio-diverse and marvelous creations ever granted the rights to this planet by their maker. And again . . . brutally and ignobly destroyed by man.

She could feel glacial tears freezing on her cheeks as her emotions remained oddly anesthetized. Finding herself descending to an exhibit, she read the signage proclaiming it to be the home of the magnificent Western Lowland Gorilla. The bitter irony was not lost on her, realizing their home *never* existed here. Sadly, home called from the vanished jungles and watery bais of Western Africa. These

15

sentient gentle great apes were mothers and fathers, babies and youngsters: families. Just like Homo sapiens, for man was a great ape too. But better, of course. Man . . . the chosen one . . . he who shall inherit the Earth. And once again, she noted frightfully to herself, man destroyed.

Her eyes glazed as she noted the complete absence of color, life or warmth around her. The horizon was a palette of black and gray barrenness, benumbing ashen hopelessness and bone-crushing godforsaken loneliness. What had happened here? Such wanton destruction.

Abby struggled, a sudden crush of emotions coalescing, too much to bear. Trying to break the grip of the tableau, she panicked; instinctively calling for her mother, *begging* for her mother. Out of her mind with grief and loss, she confused the emotions in her nightmare with the unresolved heartbreak of her mother's abrupt absence from her life. Here the nightmare always ended, leaving Abby a helpless wreck.

Without warning, Abby felt pulled away from the zoo. She beheld herself in a new and foreign environment, appearing to be a large cavern. Light shone, but the source eluded her. She felt neither warm nor cold. An enveloping layer of something soft and undulating, exuding a smell of organic dampness which clung to the walls of the cavern. How could she smell if she were dreaming?

Further down the cavern, a golden glow approached: a figure. Abby caught her breath, an unexplained premonition sending goosebumps down her arms. The emerging figure formed into that of a woman.

The alluring vision glowed with the fine golden fur draping her body. Like Abby, she sported a long mature tail with a bulbous end floating languidly around her. Her golden-white hair reached, full and glossy, down her back. A pair of exquisite wings framed her statuesque figure. From her hairline, two graceful crystal horns emerged, swirling with silver and gold liquid. Her eyes sparkled with the colors of the rainbow. She smiled benevolently at Abby. With a start, Abby realized she looked familiar. She racked her memory, but could not place the lovely face.

"My dear, we have not met. You are here because you have much to do. We are relying on you. You must save those you can. Time is short. We had hoped to do things differently. Man has conspired, fatally, to abort our plans. We must react quickly. Gather the materials you need and do the best you can."

"Madam, how am I to know what to do?"

Approaching Abby, the woman placed her hand on Abby's shoulder as her right horn split and peeled back, releasing a drop of liquid, its color flashing and filling the cavern. The woman held out her other hand to receive the drop. Reaching up to Abby's ear she placed it inside.

Disappearing, the flashing colors slowly faded as the drop moved deep into her ear. Abby's eyes closed slowly. She blinked, her eyes closing again. They finally opened with a stoic acceptance of realized purpose and clarity.

"I understand completely. I hope to see you again soon," Abby said. Taking Abby into her arms, the woman embraced her warmly.

"You will, my dear. Remember, you have Echo to aid you. I must send you back now."

"Wait. Please, who are you? What shall I call you?" The vision began to recede. She found herself in her own bed, on the verge of waking. From a great distance, she heard the woman's voice. "I was once known as Netty Doyle, my dear. You may call me Netty."

Abby gently drifted into a deep sound slumber, the details of her dream dissipating. She slept soundly.

Chapter 3

Peter pulled his BMW away from the parking lot at Sarasota Airport. He waved to Jose, who stood in line for the security bus to the check-in counter. He was anxious to board a flight to Newark which would hopefully reunite him with what was left of his family.

Peter's happiness for Scotty and Abby knew no bounds. He appreciated how long it had taken them to get this far. As he drove back into town, he observed the night life in Sarasota preparing to heat up as the party hour approached, crowds thickening on the streets. Peter had sampled very little of it, even though the venues of bars and eateries were made to order for a single man.

Some of the most predatory and beautiful women in the country flocked to Sarasota, hoping to land themselves a wealthy husband. Those were the odds any self-respecting singleton would celebrate. Even though he could now call himself well off by most standards, he normally found himself reticent to join the nightly festivities of the crazy rich in this town, and which served as a bizarre escape from the reality of the rest of the country.

But tonight he wanted to flex his muscles. Perhaps his buoyant mood, inherited from Jose's infectious happiness, portended a good omen. Taking a very deep breath, he decided: Tonight would be the night. He felt jazzed up and ready to go fishing for the ladies.

Driving down Main Street proved difficult. Traffic congestion continually hindered his efforts to find a parking place. By the time he found one, discouragement settled in, robbing him of his ebullient mood, which leaked out like a punctured tire. His reluctance to enter any of the most boisterous bars overwhelmed him. Forcing himself to suck it up, he timidly selected one which appeared more discreet and subdued.

As he entered the bar, he relaxed. The atmosphere appeared quiet and non-threatening, although clearly not the place most partiers wanted to be seen in. Definitely down scale. Oh well, it would do fine as a start for him. Scanning the bar, he noticed an empty stool between two other patrons. He started forward, but the stool was quickly taken by another man. As he stood in indecision, he noticed a couple of patrons giving him a quick once over, especially the woman. As his courage began to evaporate, one of the patrons stood up. A short dumpy man, he motioned toward him, offering his seat. Well, that was sure kind. Peter turned to thank him, but the man ducked his face down, hurrying out the door before Peter could even open his mouth.

Getting comfortable on the bar stool, he ordered a glass of wine, then glanced at his reflection in the back bar mirror. His face looked even wider and more owlish than usual. But the mirror failed to hide the quiet, clean-cut, timid man who was finally tired of being alone.

He sat, sulking about his lonely life, and ordered another glass of wine. *A little liquid courage can't hurt.* As people were coming and going, he sat stiffly on his bar stool, unsure what to do next. Feeling discouraged, he felt a bump on the right side of his stool. A patron, the woman who had been staring at him, rose from her own stool, getting ready to leave. She suddenly dropped her purse. Attempting to assist as she bent to retrieve it, they banged heads.

"Ow."

"Ouch." Peter rubbed his head, looking up into the eyes of a pretty blond woman, seemingly a few years older than him. Her nose scrunched up as she laughed heartily at her own clumsiness.

"I'm sorry, that's so typical of me. I'm rather clumsy. Are you okay?" She extended her hand to grip his arm, rubbing softly to reassure him, an intimate gesture. Touched, Peter hastened to assure her of his recovery.

"May I insist you allow me to buy you a cocktail? Just so I can assure myself you're fine?"

Her smile was so lovely, her manner so charming, that he found himself instantly enticed. *A pretty woman wants to buy me a drink. How do you like that?*

When you least expect it, something special comes your way. Looking into her relaxed and friendly face, he felt no qualms about spending time with her. All traces of nervousness disappeared. He began to relax and enjoy himself.

As the evening wore on, they discovered they had much in common. they were both from small towns, both professionals. When she found out he was an attorney, she could not resist inquiring into his intent to sue her for the knot on his noggin. She made him laugh, something unfamiliar to him.

Peter shyly suggested they have dinner together. He wanted to do anything he could to prolong their time together. He just loved how her blond curls shook as she laughed at his lame jokes. *What a doll*, he thought, enjoying how the glow of the bar lights made her eyes sparkle.

They strolled down the street just like all the other happy couples, selecting a nice restaurant, then sharing savory lobster and excellent champagne, frugality forgotten. Her hand lingered on his as she made an occasional point. Peter found himself grinning and laughing so hard the muscles in his face ached.

Finally, they realized the night must end. Suggesting she walk him to his car, she pointed out the high-rise she lived in, within easy walking distance of the restaurant. After arriving at his BMW, he inquired as to whether he could call her for dinner again. Reaching into her purse, she scribbled her cell number, clearly pleased to be asked. Placing the note in his hand, she leaned over slowly, looked into his eyes and placed her lips over his for the softest kiss he swore he would ever feel.

"Goodnight, Peter. This was wonderful. I look forward to hearing from you very soon." Turning, she disappeared into the crowd on the sidewalk.

In a daze, he drove back to Bird Key. Pulling into his driveway, he remained in the car, reliving and savoring the evening. He glowed. *Could she be any more perfect?* Looking down, he stroked the note she had given him, admiring her handwriting. Ginger Mae Shrute 914-555-0436. *How cool is that?* And off he went to bed, sleeping better than he had in years.

Ginger Mae walked quickly to the high-rise, not wanting Armoni to wait any longer than necessary. She knew he would be chewing his nails and spitting in anger because he had almost been caught when he had seen Peter walk into the bar, forcing him to make a hasty exit. They could not afford to have Peter recognize Armoni, even though they had only met briefly, months ago. Armoni knew he made an indelible impression on people.

She shook her head, amazed at the irony of the situation. Dining in elegant expensive bars and restaurants every night for months, trying to get a lead on Armoni's enemies could easily have become a drag. But how else could they hope to run into them? Sooner or later, they would show up to eat. Their excellent plan to track them back to their house where Armoni could then reclaim his property had failed to produce results. Not so excellent after all. They hadn't counted on the one night that they had decided to go to a normal, relaxed watering hole, this sudden opportunity would drop right into their laps. Armoni would be very pleased with her results.

She sighed, watching laughing couples pass her on the sidewalk, arm in arm, enjoying each other's company, just as she had enjoyed Peter's. She felt a longing for the unfamiliar life of an upstanding citizen. *Wow, where did* that *come from? Have I gotten in over my head this time?*

Her big plans for Armoni were slowly turning to ash. Sure, he had taken them to Florida, paying for everything, but he never let her out of his sight. That was not what she'd had in mind. And she could only handle his disgusting habits in small doses. She expected him to set her up in her own place, seeing her when he had the urge (she could handle that) and then get back to his life. But, it appeared, he had no life. As a matter of fact, he seemed to want to turn *her* into his life. *Ugh. Not going to happen.* She hoped that if she helped him recover his property, she could say goodbye and strike out on her own. The wealth and opportunity in Sarasota made her head spin. From the kind of men she met in the bars and clubs, she could clearly see that she and Daisy would be well able to fend on their own, without the odorous Armoni.

But she must be clever. She had come to the conclusion that Armoni kept mysterious secrets to himself. She began to suspect the veracity of his stolen property story.

And then there were his hygiene issues. A godly problem. He must have grown up with wolves. How a man could ignore simple baths, deodorant and oral care blew her mind. She had finally reached the point where she could no longer eat around him for fear of vomiting. So she just drank instead.

Fortunately, his appetite for sex had slowly mellowed. *That was bound to happen as his attention is so focused on getting his property back, thank the Lord.* And she had to consider Daisy's welfare. This was not a good environment for her. Ginger Mae regretted exposing her to Armoni, something she had always refused to do with her johns. This must end, and as soon as possible.

That's why she had said yes to dinner with Peter. She had hoped he would ask for her phone number and then a date. She could find out where he lived and where his clients lived. That should satisfy Armoni. Given enough time, she confidently planned to obtain the information Armoni constantly gnashed his teeth over. Then she would be done with this. She and Daisy would dump this smelly piece of garbage and strike out on their own.

Ginger Mae remembered the trailer trash, horse-faced, fat, little blonde in the gym at the high-rise who had happily bragged about how she had left her loser husband after she had met a wealthy guy on a website for dating millionaires. Within three weeks, she had moved into the millionaire's house. They'd been married within six months. He wasn't exactly a looker, but then, neither was she. But they were happy. What else did they need? At this point, Ginger desperately needed to grab at any straw if it aided her plan to get away from Armoni.

She had started to wonder where his money came from. It wasn't like he possessed any education or skills. Her curiosity about the people who had stolen his property increased. Now, knowing Armoni as she did, she began to have sneaking doubts about his story. After meeting Peter, she didn't think he would, in good conscience, represent thieves. But she was *damn sure* Armoni would steal bones from a puppy. Getting sucked into a crime as an accessory was nowhere on her list.

Her tired eyes flashed lightning bolts as she approached the high-rise. Looking up, she searched in vain for the seventeenth floor where they were residing. She swallowed her dread and went in to face the music.

Chapter 4

Scotty woke to find Echo's face three inches from his own, her rainbow eyes flashing spurts of gold light. *That usually means something's up*, Scotty thought. Echo held up an old fanny pack Scotty had forgotten about at least a hundred years ago.

"Where did you find that, girl?"

Echo bounced back on Scotty's stomach, getting a loud groan and a shove to the floor for her efforts. Popping back up like a yoyo, she sent her aura to Scotty. "Brother, may I have this, please, Brother? It is just what I need. I found it on the floor of your closet, under a pile of clothes, tied into a knot, covered in soil, I mean dirt, and enclosed in a tiny cardboard box that had been previously used to store blank pieces of paper that you like to use to draw pictures of animals on, until you got a new drawing device that you stick into the wall to draw with . . ."

"Okay, okay. Hush, Echo, I just woke up, give me a minute." Rolling over in bed, he glared at Echo, rubbing sleep out of his eyes. He should have known better than to ask Echo a stupid question like that. Her habit of being excessively informative and literal sometimes drove him nuts.

"Why don't you put it on, girl?" He reached out to hook it around her tiny waist. After a few adjustments, wrapping the nylon strap round and round her belly, the turquoise and gray fanny pack fit, making his somewhat scary, cuddly little buddy look like a hip, somewhat scary, cuddly, little buddy.

"What do you need a fanny pack for?"

"It is just perfect." Scrambling off Scotty's bed, Echo ran to the corner of the room where she fumbled around, returning to the bed and climbing up to sit on Scotty's stomach again.

"These are for my treasures." Echo held out her delicate leather hand revealing the plastic jar she was using to hold the hairs she had quietly plucked out of Barney last night. She shook the jar, holding it up to the light so Scotty could see the hairs.

"This is My Barney." Slipping the jar into the fanny pack, she gently gave it a pat. "My Barney will now have immortality. He will not be an Elder, but I can grow him if he dies."

Scotty's eyes bugged out. "You can *grow* him? What do you mean by that? *Immortality*? Elders have immortality? Didn't you tell us we would be Elders?"

But Echo had slipped off the bed, tired of the questions. Shuffling across the room, she threw her aura back to Scotty. "I will go find Mimi. I would like to harvest her hair, also. I am becoming quite fond of that little girl." And she was gone, leaving Scotty alone wondering if he should say anything about this to anyone. Abby would probably freak. Better keep his mouth closed for now.

A pounding on his bedroom door drew his attention. Abby poked her head in, her hair braided into pigtails.

"You up?"

"Yeah, come on in." Moving over to make room for her on his messy bed, he asked, "What's up?"

"I want you to do something for me. Feel up to a little adventure?"

Yanking on her pigtails, he nodded. "What's up with the new do, Sis?"

"It's part of my plan. Just trying it out. I want us to go into Sarasota tomorrow. I need to look low-key, don't want to draw attention to my hair. We're going to a place called the Big Cat Sanctuary. It's run by a fifth- or sixth-generation circus family. Good people. This trip is just to look around. We need to see how many animals are there. There are plans for those animals. We need to move them."

"Are you kidding me? We'd better wait until Jose returns. I don't think he'll be too keen on us going into town, Abby. He's mad enough as it is. I'd love to see the cats and all, but why do we need to move them? And how in the world do we accomplish that?"

"Fear not, little Brother. I have a plan. This is for their own good. I'll make sure the animals are handled safely. The time is getting near." Echo had quietly returned, her eyes shooting golden sparks again.

"What am I missing? Are you both in on something I don't know about? What do you mean, time is getting near?"

Abby took his face between her hands, staring intently into his golden eyes. Scotty had a premonition which told him he did not want to know any more than he already did.

"Scotty, just trust me. We're just going to take a look. Echo, it's too risky to bring you with us on this trip."

"I can transport in my automobile, Sister Abby. I have a Carriage now." Abby frowned at Scotty, her brow furrowed in question. "I won't ask."

Turning to Echo, she added, "We'll need you for the next one, Echo. I have to get everything ready first. Tonight I'm having a meeting with Peter. I'm instructing him to make arrangements to transport the animals from the port in Tampa to Newark Airport. They'll be picked up and transported to join with another convoy. We have plans for them all." Looking to Echo, the creature slowly nodded.

"How are we going to get them to Tampa? I don't doubt that Echo will make a miracle happen, but I still don't see why or how we're going to do this." It was clear to Scotty he was not going to get any more information so he tried something new. "Since we're just going to look, can I invite a guest?"

"Scotty, don't you think this trip is risky enough? Who do you want to invite?"

"Chloe. I told you about her yesterday, remember?" Abby tilted her head as if she was listening. Raising her hand, she pulled on her ear, rapidly shaking her head. Then, surprisingly, she said yes.

"But I have one condition. You must also invite Kane Cobby."

Scotty felt like a grenade ready to explode. This would count as his first date with Chloe. The possibility that he would get stuck with Kane irritated the heck out of him. He refused to do it.

"We'll leave at noon tomorrow. Make sure they're both here or I'll have to leave without you."

"But, Abby, why all the mystery? And why Kane?" Scotty tried to curb the whine in his voice.

Ignoring the question, Abby rose and left the room, Echo scampering right behind her. *That's odd. When it comes to me, Echo clings to me like an ugly babe refusing to give up her first boyfriend. So why the sudden interest in what Abby's planning to do?*

But, like most boys his age, his attention span flitted from one topic to another, easily diverted, as he grew psyched over the idea of going off the island again. Jumping into the shower to wash his fur, he wondered what he would wear to show up at Chloe's house. He knew he had better look good if they were going to let her go with them. It nagged at him that Abby had said yes so easily. It wasn't like her to let him run this risk. *Maybe Peter will talk some sense into her about her crazy plan.*

Later that morning, Scotty pulled up to the front gate of the mansion belonging to Chloe's family. A casually dressed guard in khakis and white polo shirt came to the gate after exiting a small guardhouse which matched the color of the mansion. He could see into the grounds, noting the numerous expensive vehicles parked loosely around the circular driveway. A gargantuan bronze sculpture of the ubiquitous jumping dolphins rose from a courtyard fountain.

"Hey, kid, what do you want here?" The guard was casually dismissive, probably thinking Scotty was lost. Scotty adjusted his sunglasses on his nose, feeling the late morning sun start to heat up across the back of his neck. He approached the guard.

"My name is Scotty Preston. I live on Mango Lane, on the other side of the key. I'm here to see Chloe, if she's home?" The guard said nothing, studying him thoughtfully; his eyes difficult to read through the shades he wore. Backing away from the gate, the guard returned to his shelter to use a phone, presumably to call the main house. Within two minutes, the front door opened and a five-foot whirling dervish ran toward the gate letting the front door slam thunderously behind her.

"Scotty, hi," she panted, arriving breathlessly at the gate. "Hey, can you please open this darn thing?" Stepping back, she motioned to the guard. Scotty decided to leave his Jeep parked on the side of the road and joined Chloe in walking to the house. "Did you come over to see the monkeys?"

"I'd love to see the monkeys, but I came to invite you to go to the Big Cat Sanctuary in town. We'll be leaving at noon tomorrow. I can pick you up around eleven if it's okay?" Scotty sounded wistfully earnest.

"Gee, I don't know. I'm not usually allowed to go off the island without an escort, one of the men or sometimes Mrs. Elbarad. My old nanny. If I can't go alone, would you mind if I asked her? Come on." Chloe ushered him toward the front door. "You can see the monkeys while I ask."

Scotty stepped into the cool air-conditioned foyer. He gaped at the marble floor, inset with a pastel mosaic of roses, ribbons and birds. The center of the huge foyer contained a walnut table on which lay a gilt-edged guest book. Chloe stood near the book, waving him forward, a pen in her hand.

"Hope you don't mind. It's my father's house rule. Everyone must sign in." Scotty carefully wrote his name and address on the heavy cream paper, setting the elegant Mont Blanc pen back in its holder. Looking around, he saw a double mahogany circular staircase which lost itself somewhere on the second floor. Under each elevated section of staircase he could peer into other lavish rooms. Chloe led the way through a resplendent room, dominated by a huge hand-carved stone fireplace and French doors leading to an elegant terrace overlooking an Olympic-sized pool with an unparalleled view of a luxury yacht and the Sarasota Bay glinting serenely around it.

"Come this way." Chloe motioned for him to follow her through an antechamber which opened to a small conservatory strewn with tropical plants, comfortable yellow wicker and an assortment of hand-crafted metal cages. Scotty could smell the musky organic scent of the monkeys before he saw them. He approached them slowly, not wanting to startle them. Chloe came up beside him, holding some grapes in her hand. "Here, they love these."

Scotty slowly moved from cage to cage feeding the monkeys, murmuring softly to them in delight. The monkeys moved slowly and calmly, the signs of age clear on the fur of their faces.

"How old are they?"

"I don't know. They've always been here, since I was born, and I'm almost fifteen. They can live in captivity for twenty five, thirty years. They belong to my uncle. He got them somewhere in Central America. He's around here some place. He works with my father most of the time. I hope you don't mind, he'll have to meet you since my father's not here. It's such a drag," she said, frowning. "Let me see if I can round him up, I'll be right back."

Scotty continued to observe the monkeys, remembering from rudimentary science classes the common belief that the human race somehow descended from monkeys. Well, not actual monkeys. Great apes. Humans were categorized as great apes. It was said that 96-98 percent of human DNA matched that of chimpanzees. But there was still the great story of the missing link. Many primates were thought to be our cousins, but science still could not find the direct link on the tree of evolution from which humans descended. One of science's enduring enigmas.

"Well, young man, it is my pleasure to meet you." Jumping up, Scotty extended his hand as Chloe's uncle walked into the room. Behind him, an older woman eyed Scotty from behind heavy horn-rimmed reading glasses, her wrinkled face set in a suspicious glare. Chloe reached out to drag her out from behind her uncle.

"Relax, Mrs. Elbarad, Scotty is my friend."

Everyone took a chair, Chloe sitting as close to Scotty as she could, doing nothing to dispel the feeling he was facing a firing squad.

"Well," Scotty said, squirming in his chair.

"Well," Chloe's uncle said, his leg swinging placidly, admiring his own expertly tooled riding boots, a smile on his aristocratic well-tanned face.

"My dear boy, Chloe wants very much to attend this outing with you," Mrs. Elbarad cleared her throat, taking command of the situation. "I would be more comfortable if I was able to meet your mother."

Scotty's eyes fell. "My mother is dead, madam. Killed last year in an auto accident. That's why we moved to Sarasota. My dad left us when I was a child. I live with my older sister and her boyfriend, a close family friend. My sister is taking us to the sanctuary. Oh." Turning to Chloe he said, "I forgot to tell you. My sister suggested I invite Kane Cobby. Do you know him?"

Chloe's uncle interrupted. "Captain Cobby's boy? Yes, I know the family. Captain Cobby is a good man. I know something of the story behind his boy's difficult life before his mother walked out."

"Oh, good, then it's settled. Scotty, you can pick us up at eleven."

Glancing at Mrs. Elbarad, he saw the woman nod, giving Scotty a stingy smile.

Jumping up, Chloe announced she would walk Scotty to the door. From the other room they could hear the sound of a tinny lawnmower getting closer. Before he knew what had hit him, Scotty was assailed by the tiny body of a soapy, soaking wet Teddy. The diminutive dog shook himself, suds flying in all directions, accompanied by laughter and scrambling. The groomer entered the room, profusely apologizing with a towel in his hand. But Teddy, determined to elude him, flew off Scotty's lap to dash first to Chloe, then Mrs. Elbarad's lap, soaking them all. Grabbing the towel from the groomer, Scotty managed to scoop up Teddy, his eager face alive with mischief, his Lilliputian pink tongue flicking furiously, alert for any chance to grab more attention. Handing the canine monkey back to the groomer, Scotty and Chloe made a hasty exit.

Walking with Chloe to the gate, Scotty asked her if she knew Kane.

"Yeah, he's been around the neighborhood for quite a while. We all kind of know one another."

"I'm heading over to see him now. See you tomorrow." Turning, he gave Chloe a wave, hopped into his Jeep and sped down the road to confront Kane. *Why in the world Abby's forcing this on me sure beats all.* He wondered about the revelation that Kane had been deserted by his mother. Sounded like a story there. Abby probably knew the scoop. Funny, he realized almost everyone in his life came from a broken family. They all knew pain and rejection well, especially Jose.

Thinking about Chloe, he wondered what her father did for a living. Must be a pretty rich dude to afford a house like that. He knew it must be hard on Chloe, losing her mother to some freak illness and her father never being around. Well, she could join the club. Hopefully, she wouldn't mind lowering her standards to give him a tumble. He wondered how well Kane knew her. Maybe he *could* be a little more patient with him, now that he understood where the chip on his shoulder came from.

Arriving home, he ran down to the dock. The deserted yacht rocked gently in its mooring with Captain Cobby nowhere to be seen. Shouting from the dock, he asked for permission to board, just to be sure. He felt ridiculous, but his sister insisted. According to her, to do otherwise would be rude, even though, technically, they owned the vessel. While the captain maintained a presence onboard, the traditional nicety sufficed, extended out of courtesy.

Sprinting back to the house, he rifled through the kitchen drawers looking for paper and pencil. Taking his time, he composed a friendly invitation to the sanctuary for Kane, closing with a comment about how Chloe was coming too and they could all have fun together. He knew it sounded lame but it should do the job.

Ambling back down to the dock, with his posse now tagging along—except for Echo, missing in action again—he left the note where Kane would be sure to see it.

Returning to the house from the dock, he felt the oppressive weight of the sun. His shirt lay plastered to his back, his tail limp and strangled, wrapped unnaturally around his waist. He really needed a soothing dip in the pool. Looking down at the hot panting faces of Penny, Mimi, and Barney—*how come he isn't with Echo?*—he decided they could use a dip too. Their panting was driving him crazy. Whipping off his sunglasses, he ran to the pool.

"Last one in gets dog food for dinner." Ripping off his shirt before he jumped in, he somehow missed the sight of Kane walking from the carriage house next door, on his way to the dock. Had he seen Kane, he would have wondered, for a split second, if his flashing golden eyes could be seen from the yacht, or if his tawny golden six-foot tail could be seen, or even the beginnings of what were clearly going to be wings. Yes, he would definitely have wondered.

Chapter 5

Abby spent the day resting, although she didn't feel tired. For some reason, Echo continued to dog her steps all day long, even when she tried to rest up. She figured she must have slept for four hours, although she could have sworn it was only fifteen minutes. *Where did my mind go for the last four hours?* She had no memory of sleeping. Echo lay on the bed with her, by her side, both of them with their wings crushed beneath them. Hardly comfortable. *So how did I fall asleep?*

Glancing at the clock again, she remembered her date with Peter. Admonishing Echo to stay home until she signaled for her, she tucked her tail securely away, hurrying over to his house.

Echo sat upright against Abby's pillows as Abby hurried out of the bedroom to keep her meeting with Peter. Out of the corner of her eye, she noticed the comforter slide off the side of the bed as a golden creature with rainbow eyes slid atop the bed to plunk down in front of Echo. The two creatures stared at one another as their auras spoke, twin wise furry cat faces looking like bookends.

"Echo, I think you need to keep your eye on Abby. She is going to need your help more than you know." Netty sat at the edge of the bed, watching the two minions silently communicate.

Echo reached into her fanny pack to pull out the bottles of hair she had removed from Barney and Mimi, silently passing it to the other minion. She hung her head. "Are you sure—My Barney?" The auras dimmed.

Netty nodded, rising from the bed. She held her arms out for the other creature. "We will do the best we can. Come, Baby, time to get home to Wil." She bent down to stroke Echo. "We will see you soon." Straightening up, she held Baby to her breast and disappeared in a flurry of thin air and golden wings as Echo slid off the bed to head to Peter's house.

Ringing Peter's doorbell, Abby thought she heard voices, the sound of laughter. Definitely an unusual occurrence as Peter generally cultivated a quiet and stoic personality. Her curiosity aroused, she rang the doorbell again. The door opened suddenly, showing Peter standing in the entrance, his face flushed and smiling.

"Abby, what a nice surprise. Please come in." He took her hand, drawing her into the room as she heard soft music coming from the sound system. Italian? He ushered her into the kitchen, suddenly shy.

"Abby, I would like you to meet a friend of mine. This is Ginger Mae Shrute. Ginger, this is my friend and employer, Abby Preston." A very attractive blonde stood up from the kitchen table, her eyes unable to hide her intense curiosity. Peter went over to her, placing his arm around her shoulders. She looked at him, smiling.

This is obviously not just a friendly relationship, Abby realized with a start. Looking around the kitchen, the makings of a romantic dinner lay scattered over the granite countertops. *Lobster and champagne?* She raised her eyebrows in confusion. "Are you celebrating something?"

Peter hustled over to Abby, pulling out a chair. "Please, have a seat, Abby. Would you care for a cocktail?" Abby declined, keeping her eyes on Ms. Shrute. "Ginger and I aren't celebrating anything special. This just happens to be two of her favorite things."

I'll bet, Abby thought. She watched Ginger simper as Peter refilled her champagne glass. The woman was clearly older than Peter. Why that should bother her, she didn't know. Jose was younger than her, yet she thought nothing of it.

"So, Ginger, are you from Sarasota?"

"Ginger *Mae.* No, I'm from New York. I moved here a few months ago." Fluffing her hair distractedly, she continued, "I love it here. My niece, Daisy, lives with me. I thought this climate would be good for her. She's mute." Ginger Mae cast her eyes down as she spoke Daisy's name.

"I'm so sorry to hear that." Abby absorbed an uncomfortable impression from Ginger Mae. *Desperation? Yes.* And cunning, quite subliminal. Making a note to herself, she decided Ms. Shrute would bear some watching. Rising, she directed herself to Peter.

"I hope you don't mind. Can I have a word with you . . . privately?" Unable to help herself, she threw a tight dismissive glance toward the woman. Ginger Mae picked up her champagne glass, smiling at Peter.

"Don't worry about me, hon. I'll just go out to the pool. Take all the time you need. Nice meeting you, Abby. I'm sure we'll meet again." She gave Peter a kiss on the cheek and sashayed out the door.

Abby turned to Peter, noting his red face and bashful grin, irritatingly simple. She caught herself. *Wow, my claws are out. Could I be jealous?* Abby realized she'd been the only female on the scene for some time now. She gladly welcomed another female presence—Echo didn't count—as she could sure use a girlfriend. But she instinctively knew Ginger Mae wasn't girlfriend material. She just didn't know why. Dismissing the enigma of Ginger Mae Shrute, she turned to Peter, all business.

"I have a strange request for you, although I'm not at liberty to explain why I need the things you'll help me obtain. Trust me that it's urgent. I'll make everything clear to you in time. First I need you to employ the services of a dozen truckers with vehicles capable of safely carrying wild animals. Their trip will be short, loading no problem. My concern is the heat and proper ventilation. The transport is for one hour. Water won't be needed. The men must be reliable and competent. I need them to be available within two weeks. I know that will make your job more difficult. If need be, I'll reimburse them for any previous commitment, with a significant bonus for themselves, of course. I don't care what I must spend to make this happen.

"The pickup is here, in Sarasota. They're not to know the exact location until minutes before the pickup. Please find hotels for the drivers and their trucks. I don't want more than two truckers to stay in the same hotel." Peter furiously took notes, his eyebrows raised, his brow furrowed.

"This next request is more difficult. I'll need fifty drivers and trucks in the same amount of time. The haul will be longer. About two hours. The loading is more difficult . . . just unwieldy terrain. Again, the animals will be no problem. But make no mistake, this will be a herculean task. The difficulty arises at our destination. Again, difficult topography.

"I'll also need five trucks capable of transporting elephants and four giraffes. Plus trucks capable of handling aquatic animals. I need a complete list of everyone employed at the Bronx Zoo in New York City. They'll be quietly offered bonuses for their expertise regarding transport of their charges." At that, Peter's jaw dropped. He stared at Abby, ready with a question. She held up her finger to her lips.

"Not yet. There's more. I need all the drivers from the second group to be single, with no attachments to family. They must be law abiding. No felons, absolutely no violent crime. I want you to hire the investigators who found Mama Diaz. It will be their responsibility to vet the drivers. I want all drivers who have any personal pets to be encouraged to bring them. Pets of any kind. Provisions will be made to accommodate any unusual pets beyond the normal dogs and cats." Abby paused, the strain in her voice unmistakable. Her sunglasses slipped down her nose revealing a golden glow around the spaces between the glasses and her face. Her finger pushed the shades back into place. She glanced at Peter to gauge his reaction. His face had drained of all color.

"Peter, do you trust me?" Abby covered his hand with her own.

"Absolutely, I do." His voice faltered, confusion ripping across his face.

"I need your faith in me more than ever." Bowing her head, she quickly strategized. *How much can I tell him without freaking him out? He does have a right to know. More than anyone.* She knew an easier way to force him to do her bidding, but if she chose that path he would probably never forgive her. She knew it would be better if he cooperated of his own volition. If she told him too much, he may shut down in shock. She needed his analytical non-emotional mind to pull all this together.

"I want you to also arrange transportation on a private airfreight flight from Tampa to Newark Airport for the Sarasota animals. I'll need extra trucks with the appropriate accommodations, water included this time. They'll be transported along with the group from the zoo. I'll be at the zoo myself, along with everyone here at our compound, including you. Please arrange for our flights from Tampa to Newark. I think it would be best if you charter a private jet. All our dogs will be coming, of course."

"Abby, I don't understand. This is an enormous undertaking. I can't make this happen in two weeks." Peter withdrew a white handkerchief from his pocket and wiped his brow, his expression grave. Standing, he took a quick gulp of water from the tap, then turned to Abby, his face pale and leached of all color.

"What you are asking is illegal. Do you have permission to take these animals? And why would you want to? If you have a fascination for wildlife, there are other ways we can explore this. What about the safety of the animals and the people in their proximity? Abby, I don't know." Shaking his head, he began to pace. Abby saw him glance out to the pool where Ginger Mae waited. Rising, she fixed him with an icy glare.

"Perhaps I have made a mistake. I thought you would be up to the task. I understand the timing is difficult for you." Softening, she went to him, placing her hand on his cheek. "Would it help if we hired Ginger Mae to help you? We can have her deal with the temp agencies. Of course you will need a staff to handle the paperwork and organization." She really did not want to have that woman around, emanating her bad vibe. But right now, Peter was more important to her. She wanted to avoid having Echo subdue him at all costs. Observing his expression, she could tell he was conflicted, clearly making emotional calculations. Hmm . . . that was so unlike him. Perhaps she had underestimated his connection with this woman.

"Peter?"

"I just don't think I can commit to something this fraught with danger. Maybe if I had more time. Abby, you know I don't want to say no to you." Abby's hand slipped down to her side, defeat weighing her down.

"I'm so sorry, Peter, you leave me no choice. This is not what I wanted."

Turning, she purposely hurried across the foyer floor to Peter's front door as he trailed behind, still apologizing. Abby opened the door to find Echo awaiting her. Stepping aside, she let Peter see.

"What the heck is this?" Peter looked up, astonished but not frightened. *Good, it will go smoother that way*, she thought. With a nod to Echo, Abby stepped back toward the kitchen to keep an eye on Ginger Mae, still relaxing by the pool.

"Abby, what's going on here?" His head swiveled to her then back to the front door. "What the hell is this thing?"

"It's okay, Peter. This won't take long." Abby watched as Echo entered the foyer, a crystal antler splitting open. With a last glance toward the pool, she approached Echo, holding out her arm. A tiny blood-red circle dropped into her trembling hand. Moving over to a transfixed Peter, his owl eyes nearly bursting, she raised her hand. The tiny drop of red liquid launched itself, disappearing deep into his ear canal.

He frantically brushed at his ear, his efforts ineffectual. Movements slowed as the effect of the red drop became apparent. His eyes closed slowly, blinked, then closed again. They flew open, color coming back and a smile lighting up his face as if nothing untoward had happened. He didn't even comment on Echo's presence.

"You can leave now, Echo, thank you." She picked Echo up, giving her a hug and a kiss, whispered, "I love you," then closed the door behind her. Turning back to Peter, she repeated the instructions she had given him in the kitchen.

"I'll get right on it, Abby. Let me talk to Ginger Mae straight away." His face showed nothing but eagerness.

"Careful now, she is not to know any of the details of the mission, is that clear?"

Patting her on the shoulder, Peter assured her of his discretion. Doubting nothing, Abby left, confident her plans were now underway.

Ginger Mae kissed Peter goodbye at the front door, her anxiousness and fear of Armoni holding her in an iron grip, a definite damper on her evening. She was running very late and Armoni would have her scalp. Stifling her trepidation, she concentrated on Peter, who gazed up at her like a grinning fool. *For God's sake, he's acting like this is the first time he's ever had sex.*

"Are you sure you won't need me to pick up your things tomorrow? I can send a car for you and Daisy if it will be easier."

She was convinced Peter would jump off the Ringling Bridge if she asked him to. "I think that would be very helpful, thank you. I can't wait for you to meet Daisy. Are you sure she won't be in the way?" Ginger Mae held her breath. She didn't want Peter to change his mind. Making Daisy safe was always her first concern.

"Sweetheart, there's plenty of room for everyone in this big house. You'll be spending a lot of time here anyway. I'll prepare a room for her in the morning."

Looking up at the sky, they could see the sun starting to dispel the darkness, tendrils of a new day preparing to announce supremacy over the night. "I guess it *is* tomorrow already. I'll let you go. This is going to be a difficult day—we have so much to do for Abby. I'm glad you're willing to help us. It'll be a perfect way for you to get to know the family." He swept a piece of her hair away from her face.

"And to get to know you better." Glancing outside, she saw the car Peter had ordered pull into the driveway. "I'll call you as soon as I'm ready." Thinking better of that, she then suggested he have the car ready in two hours. Anticipating trouble, she decided to make a quick getaway. It might be better if they sneaked out while Armoni slept.

On the way back to the high-rise, she plotted her escape, her thoughts then turning to Ms. Abby Preston. She had sensed the tension in Abby, surmising she might be part of the cause. She wasn't sure if Ms. Abby had bought her act or not. She had seemed quite surprised to find her there, in her cool character kind of way. Ginger Mae could handle a female with a snippy attitude just fine, having no intention of letting any woman come between her and her plans.

What an astonishing surprise, to have Peter offer her a job. With Abby's approval no less. And he sweetened it further by suggesting she move in. Although it was supposed to be for the duration of the project, she had no doubt she could make it permanent, getting swept away with the idea of becoming the mistress of Peter's fabulous home. He wasn't a bad guy to sleep with either. A little on the tentative side for her taste, but that would change as he became more confident with her. Actually, he really was a gentleman. The age difference was not a problem for her, a nice change from all the imperious older johns, with their grasping fingers and harsh demands. *Gosh, this could be a real dream for me and Daisy.*

And then she came crashing down, fast. She reminded herself: Armoni would go berserk. She was more than an investment in his scheme. She had convinced him she cared for him. No man would take this lying down. She wondered how an unstable ignorant one would take it. She felt in her purse for her blade. Having to use it would be dangerous. She could not afford to get herself embroiled in anything sordid, her relationship with Peter still too new for him to be fully invested in her. She doubted he would be able to afford the complication to his life right now. As they say, timing is everything. She must sneak out of the high-rise without trouble. She knew Armoni would have a difficult time finding her since Peter had sent a car for her, leaving him in the dark about her destination. By the time Armoni was able to track her, she would have worked her magic on Peter, maybe even telling him some of the truth. Just in case.

Feeling more confident, she watched the sun come up, praying for an omen to bless her plans. As the car approached the high-rise, she asked the driver to wait, informing him she planned to send a child down to the car to wait for her. If there was any problem, he was to take the child to Bird Key where he had picked her up. She gave him Peter's cell number, asking him to relay the change of plans.

Her heart beating wildly, she rode the elevator to the seventeenth floor. Getting out of the elevator, she put her hands to her face, trying to calm herself down. Her blood pounded so hard at her temples she thought it would wake the neighbors. Standing in front of their condo, she listened carefully, hearing nothing. She eased open the door and slipped in. Looking around at the mess on the floor, her heart almost stopped as she spied Armoni, his back against the refrigerator, sitting on the floor, asleep. His head rested on his chest, a bottle of gin in his lap, his face and shirt crusted with sauce from some mystery food item. Eyeing the empty gin bottle, she knew he would be violent if he woke before she made her escape.

Tip-toeing to Daisy's bedroom, she woke the child, quietly instructing her to put on her robe and slippers. She put some clothes in a small travel bag and stole to the bedroom she shared with Armoni. Looking wildly around the mess, she spied a large piece of her luggage. Opening it up, she began stuffing clothes and shoes into the bag. On the dresser sat Armoni's wallet. Picking it up, she hit pay dirt, stuffing a wad of bills into her pocket. Leaving some items behind, she hurried to Daisy's bedroom where she found Daisy sitting on the bed with her bag and her stuffed dog. Slipping both bags over her shoulder, she put her fingers to her lips. Taking Daisy's hand they hurried past Armoni, still asleep on the floor in the kitchen. Outside the condo, she didn't breathe until they were on the way down in the elevator. She tried to catch her breath, her underarms soaked from the tension as she hustled them into the car. Daisy stared at her calmly, her eyes missing nothing. Leaning back in her seat, Ginger Mae wrapped her arms around the child, holding her close. She felt Daisy relax.

"Don't you worry, baby doll, we have nowhere to go but up now." Holding Daisy, Ginger Mae slept all the way to Peter's house, where she woke to a tap on the window. They looked up to see Peter's welcoming grin, his generous arms wide open. For now, they were safe.

His own snoring woke him. He lay on the floor not wanting to move, trying to remember why he wasn't in bed. His mouth tasted like dry dog shit. Realizing his nose lay buried in his armpit, he gagged on the foul odor. He desperately needed some water. His throat was dry but his head hurt too much to move. Where was Ginger Mae?

"Ginger Mae, git me some water, right now!" Remembering he had got drunk because she hadn't come home after dinner last night, he struggled weakly to his feet. *That bitch. Partying it up with the enemy.* He hadn't liked the idea of her going over there to begin with. He didn't even actually know where she was. Good thing too, or he would have gone over there and yanked her out by her hair. He imagined the gay blade's hands on his Ginger Mae and he saw red.

"Ginger Mae!" *Where was that bitch*? He leaned over the faucet, letting the water run into his mouth. Swallowing, he looked at his watch. It was almost noon. Wow. He had been out for a long time. No wonder his neck hurt like a damn. He better go lie down. *Why didn't that bitch wake me up when she got home?*

Passing Daisy's room, he saw the door was open. He stumbled in, his bleary eyes trying to focus. Her room looked different, kinda empty. *What was up with that?* Stumbling to his own bedroom, he slammed the door against the wall, the doorknob punching a hole in the sheetrock. *Whoops.* He tried to focus on the bed, his eyes bloodshot and useless. "Ginger Mae," he shouted, making his head pound. Wincing, he toned it down. Trying again, he collapsed on the bed, his hands searching for her.

"Come on, babe, wake the fuck up and take care of me." It occurred to him that she might be playing with him. She was probably mad at him for falling asleep in the kitchen. *When she came home, she was probably looking forward to some good bangin' after hanging out with the fag lawyer.* Feeling around the bed, it finally sunk in that she wasn't there. Groaning, he rolled over and held his head, thinking that all he needed was a good fuck to clear his head. Tugging at his pants seemed to take forever. He pulled off his three-day-old underwear, slinging the foul garment across the room, wondering why he had to take care of himself when he was supporting a hot juicy blonde who seemed to increasingly avoid having sex with him. *The selfish bitch.*

How would she like it if I climbed into bed with tight, young Daisy? Yeah, he had seen her watching him in the morning when he took a quick naked run to the kitchen for his morning Budweiser. *She probably wants me, just like Kelly did when she was that age. They all want it, the sluts. I've left her alone so far out of respect for my love for Ginger Mae, but what the heck—I'm mad at her anyway. Would serve her right.* He could handle them both no problem. Mumbling to himself, he drooled on the comforter and fell back to sleep.

Chapter 6

Lita had come to New York City at the request of her superior at the CIA. It was a treat to get away from Sarasota where she had to be constantly on guard. Today she sported a trim linen pantsuit and low heels. Her riotous curls were tamed and pulled back in a sleek ponytail. Her exotic face was devoid of all makeup, save a touch of coral lip balm. Her beauty didn't need enhancement, but her role as Nasir's mistress demanded it.

She watched the city bustle with commuters, all leading busy lives, hurrying home to their loved ones. With a pang, she realized she envied them. A highly charged and committed agent since college, she'd had her share of suitors over the years but found she was already married to her country. After seven years of playing such an isolating role in the sunshine state, she was surprised to see herself resetting her priorities. Now in her mid-thirties, her biological clock had started to tick loud enough to be heard over the clink of cocktail glasses and seductive bedroom music.

As much as she felt excited to be in New York, she wondered why she received the call in to headquarters. Something must be up, although she had no idea what it could be. Things were moving as planned on her end. She was in the process of packing her house and relocating to Washington D.C., and Omar had convinced her (as if she would refuse) to take a swank job in Washington to be close to him. Clearly, his triumph in the election would be inevitable. He had hinted to her that his plans included her coming out of the shadows and taking a more visible role in his life. The thought of what that meant long-term made her sick. She doubted how much longer she could conceal her contempt.

Lita stopped on the sidewalk, pulling her coat closer as the late spring winds whipped through the tunnels created by the monolithic office buildings standing like proud stoic soldiers over the hard electric grittiness of her surroundings. Pushing on, she took a turn off the main thoroughfare, her destination a tiny storefront Asian market with trays of tempting colorful citrus and greens that blocked the sidewalk.

Habit forced her to glance around behind her, noting a mother dragging two children with schoolbooks, their laughing faces full of the promise a new day brings. Across the street an older man, dressed poorly for the blustery weather, chased a hat down the street, meeting her eyes briefly as he scooped it up and turned back, a camera in hand. Delivery men in double-parked vans carried goods into other storefronts while garbage cans were noisily placed at the curb for pick up. Distracted by her curious summons, she decided she went unnoticed.

Ducking into the grocery, she made her way through the cramped rows of food stuffs, the cool smells of sharp freshness a contrast to the vague rotting smell on the street. She stepped through a small plastic doorway where she found young Asian men cleaning produce for the front of the store. They nodded, unsmiling, and continued their work. She found a wide passageway off a storeroom in the very back of the store which led to a metal door, no doorknob in evidence. An electronic key lock stood guard on the wall. Taking out her passkey she swiped it, hearing the door pop open. As she passed through, she waved up at the sophisticated surveillance system, the door automatically locking behind her.

Two hours later, she sat in the conference room of her supervisor's offices, surrounded by eight other men and women from her original team. They had known one another for over a decade. All were trusted and committed agents, willing to sacrifice their lives to preserve the quickly eroding freedoms of the beloved country they hardly recognized anymore.

Looking around the table, Lita observed the shock on their faces as they learned they were all being reassigned, including Lita. Reassignment folders passed around the table, but there was nothing for Lita. Her heart hammering, she wondered what had happened. It was unlikely the agents would be told anything, explanations from their superiors were never obligatory. They would just have to follow the story in the news media like the rest of the country. Eventually bits and pieces of the truth would trickle down through the ranks, just as in any other company. But why no assignment for her? Her fellow agents prepared to leave.

A few were making plans to meet at a local hangout across town. Lita was asked to join them. Nodding her head, she caught the eye of her supervisor, receiving a subtle nod, permission to stay behind. Explaining she would catch up at the bar and grill, she said goodbye to her team and returned to her seat at the table.

"Okay, let's hear it." Lita's supervisor, William Martin, was a blandly handsome man who had done his training with her after graduating from a mid-western university known for its football successes. One of the good ole boys, he rose quickly, easily promoted from within the ranks, leaving Lita his subordinate. The fact that they once shared a short affair during their training had luckily escaped the eyes of all at the company.

Coming over to sit next to her at the table, he placed his hands atop hers.

"I know this has been hard on you, Lita. I should think you would be happy it's over."

"What do you mean *over*, William, he's still out there, and he'll still win the election. That means the Salafis have won." Her tone turned to bitterness; confusion and hostility turning her face ugly. Unexpectedly, she burst into tears. She wiped her nose, humiliated by her show of emotion, abjectly unprofessional. "I'm so sorry, William, it's just that I feel like the last decade of my life has been flushed down the toilet."

William rose, pulling Lita to her feet. He put his arms around her and kissed the top of her head. They stood holding each other until Lita calmed down. Releasing her, he stepped back.

"Don't you know by now that I'll look after you? I know you, of all people, are entitled to an explanation. I don't have much that will make you feel good though. We've failed to get any direct evidence on Omar or his mosque. We know from the Net and informants that they're definitely planning something. We believe it will involve a bomb of a catastrophic nature. We don't know when or where. We've heard from our team in China that they're paranoid about becoming a target now they're the world's leading economy. But you know all of that. Two things have happened since we last talked. China seems to be under the impression that it's the U.S. who's conspiring to destroy their economy, in retaliation for bringing the West to its knees."

Lita opened her mouth to hotly object, but William cut her off.

"I know, I know. It doesn't make sense, clearly both countries benefit from a cordial relationship. We've come to believe they're being fed false intelligence by the Salafis through indirect believable sources. The small plot we stumbled on over a decade ago is suddenly taking on more ominous considerations, if you're not too timid to connect the dots. Our current cowardly administration is running scared. They know they're going to lose the election. The senior administration staff is scrambling for comfortable exits. It's time to start covering all those expensive Socialist New World asses.

"That brings me to the second thing, which is why our mission has been scrubbed. They don't want any evidence of this investigation to fall into the hands of the new cabinet members in Omar's administration. The shredding is occurring as I speak. The last thing the current administration needs is a global scandal to put the damper on the new careers of the administration hacks, and the President, of course. There is no telling how seriously it would impact the fees he'll receive for global speaking engagements. And how will his sycophants be able to sell access to the White House if they're blamed for trying to use the CIA to bring the new president down, spying on him for over a decade? The liberal press would run with that story for years."

"We can't let them get away with this," Lita cried passionately. William shook his head, the born survivor of several administrations.

"Save your energy and your emotions, Lita. It's done. The only thing I can offer you is your new assignment. You're ordered to report to this office within one month. That should give you enough time to put this behind you."

Handing her a file card, he continued, "You are to have your possessions shipped to your new address in Norwalk, Connecticut. I think you'll be pleased." William finally smiled. "It's a lovely town that has successfully protected its residents from the onslaught of the tenement invasion which has destroyed so many of our cities. Much like Sarasota was able to do.

"You'll report to me. I'm putting you in charge of a team that will be tasked with coordinating data from our overseas operatives with data collected here at home. You, and only you, will be quietly looking for more evidence to support what we now suspect will involve China, or any other group for that matter, with the Salafis. No one on your team is to know who your target is. Best of all, your private life will be your own from now on."

Lita sat stunned, her conflicted emotions preventing rational thought. She took a deep breath, trying to clear her head. At the moment all she could focus on was 'your private life will be your own from now on'. No more of Omar's sexual brutality. No more hiding who she really was. She could have actual friends, maybe a boyfriend.

"Did I not mention this was a promotion?"

Finally, William's words put a wry smile on her face. "Expense account?"

"Yes."

"Budget for my new office, with a window, of course?"

"Yes."

"My own secretary . . . that I don't have to share?"

William smiled. "Yes."

"Personal driver?"

"Emphatically, no." They laughed together, knowing the system was not perfect but they had to do their best anyway. She would be okay.

Thanking William, she promised to stay in touch. She knew she would make a philosophical adjustment and accept what had happened. Now she was just anxious to get to the restaurant to meet the rest of the team for a little R & R.

Chapter 7

Omar tossed his briefcase on the black and maroon spread on his bed. Slipping off his Italian loafers, he opened his closet door, looking for the clothes that would be just right to complete the disguise he would be forced to wear to the mosque this evening. He resented the call ordering him back to Sarasota. His frantic schedule allowed little room for deviations. He flew all over the U.S. for rallies and fundraisers and this would set his schedule back unnecessarily. His team freaked out, screaming bloody murder because of the cancelations he had forced them to make.

It was inexcusable for the imams to do this to him at this late date. They were too close to screw up now. The polls loved him and his numbers were still rising. Even faster since the elusive Mrs. Jane Nasir had mysteriously died. Patting himself metaphorically on the shoulder, he chuckled at what a genius call he had made. His good mood died as he pondered the reasons he could have been called back to the mosque. None of them qualified as urgent enough to warrant this kind of action.

He laid out his clothes carefully, hoping he could squeeze in the time to look in on his daughter. She would hear that he was home eventually. He didn't want her hurt by his inattention. Pressing a bell, he ordered a cup of tea to be delivered to his daughter's room for him to enjoy as he surprised her with his visit.

Making his way to his daughter's bedroom, his other cellphone rang; a throwaway that he changed every week. Only one person knew this number. Glancing at the cell, he recognized his contact's number. After a brief conversation, he hung up. The meeting was not for two weeks. *Two goddamn weeks.* Sounding evasive, his contact reported something serious was up. Omar was ordered to do nothing until contacted. *Nothing?* His contact expressly ordered him to stay in Sarasota. Omar objected to the chaos it would cause his campaign. His staff would flip out, the press would go nuts. "Unavoidable" was the response.

Omar racked his memory, looking for something that the imams may have objected to. He dismissed the thought, knowing his performance to have been flawless.

Finding some unexpected available time on his hands, he smiled. He knew one person who would be overjoyed to see him. Dialing Lita's cell, he heard her pick up.

"Darling, how would you like to have dinner tonight in your favorite restaurant and a night of lovemaking that will last until the sun comes up?"

"Omar, I thought you were in Texas. Don't you have a fundraiser tonight?" Lita sounded a little stressed, delight absent from her voice.

"What's wrong, darling? You don't sound like yourself." Omar's short temper was well known and this was the last thing he expected from his mistress. *Potential wife*, he corrected himself, although he had yet to set that plan in motion.

"I'm sorry, Omar, I'm just tired from all the packing I've been doing the last few weeks." Mollified, Omar thought she sounded much better.

"Well, perhaps we should stay in. You can cook for me instead."

"No, no, I would love to go out. It would be a lovely break. Besides, the house is a mess. I've packed so much I don't think you'll be comfortable anymore. And the bedroom is the worst."

"Okay, my love. You win. I want you to pack a bag for at least a week, maybe more. I'll get us a suite at the Ritz Carlton. We'll have plenty of privacy and be quite comfortable."

There was a pause and Omar could almost hear her thinking on the other end. *What is there to think about?* he wondered impatiently. This was not like Lita at all.

"Darling, I hate to take you away from the campaign at such an important juncture. This is a critical time. Why would you want to risk anything now? You're so close." She sounded breathless.

"Darling, are you alone? Did I call at the wrong time?" His voice cut like a steel knife.

"My love, you know I exist only for you. I'm only thinking of your welfare. I'm honored by your call. I'll pack a bag immediately." Hanging up satisfied, Omar felt a thrill as he thought of the intense sex he would enjoy for the next few days. Lita was an unquenchable lover. He laughed confidently to himself. He would do his utmost to ensure she was satisfied, as always.

With a smile on his face, he proceeded to his daughter's bedroom. He wondered if he could arrange a few fundraisers at the Ritz, something exclusive, while he waited for the imams to meet with him, something big to pull his butt out of the fire.

Picking up his business cell, he instructed Andrew to contact his campaign manager with the change of plans. He also instructed him to make reservations for the Ritz Carlton, under the name of Mr. and Mrs. Brooks. "Please mention they will be checking in through the private entrance," he added.

Concluding the call, he knocked at his daughter's door, hearing laughter. The door opened and the apple of her daddy's eye appeared, throwing herself into her father's arms, erasing all of his nagging anxiety.

Chapter 8

Scotty rose bright and early today—the big day. His excitement percolated contagiously as the posse sensed something good afoot. Their eager faces shined with false expectation of being included. Noticing that Echo was nowhere in the room, Scotty peered out the window, frowning at the sky: overcast and threatening rain. Having neglected to check the forecast, he sorted through his gadgets until he located one which would give him the weather report. Intermittent showers. Well, that wouldn't stop him.

Looking through his closet, he searched for a shirt which would conceal his wings. His tail twitched sharply as if it heard his thoughts. Spotting his windbreaker, he slid it over his messy hair, the hood hanging down, beautifully covering the bulge of his growing wings. Maybe the intemperate weather would serve a purpose after all.

Running down the stairs, Barney and Mimi yipping at his heels and Penny descending like a regal queen, he found Abby at the breakfast table, Echo sitting on top facing her. It felt like they were brainstorming, fleeting auras stroked his mind then dissipated. Not enough to tell him what they were talking about. He looked for dog food while he watched Echo climb down from the table to take her spot next to Barney. Barney had been very chummy with Penny and Mimi of late. Probably a result of all of Echo's unexplained absences. Mimi only had food on her mind as she pawed the back of Scotty's legs, urging him to hurry. Filling their bowls with fresh water, he turned to Abby, who appeared lost in thought.

"Hey, Ab, you excited about the trip to the sanctuary?" Scotty thought Abby didn't seem too happy.

She turned, absently giving him a smile. "Sorry, kiddo, I was just wondering about Jose. I haven't heard from him since he landed in Newark and left to meet the investigators." Rising, she added, "I think I'll try to reach him before we leave. Did you speak to Kane?"

"Not exactly. He wasn't on the boat so I left him a note. After I finish with the dogs, I'm going to run down to the dock and look him up. Then I'm going over to Chloe's to pick her and her babysitter up."

"Babysitter?" Abby didn't sound like she was in the mood for a joke right now. Looking closer, he could see lines on her brow and signs of weariness under her eyes. Even her tail looked dispirited and droopy today.

"Just kidding. She had to agree to have her old nanny come with us or she couldn't go. You think our house is nice, you should see hers. They have guards at the gate and a cook with a staff. Her father travels a lot for business. He's not around much. Her mother died a while ago, so her nanny and her uncle look after her. She's lonely, I guess. By the way, she's also really pretty." He paused, looking at his sister. "Abby, is there something you want to tell me? You look like hell."

She frowned and raised an eyebrow at him. Scotty raised his hands. "Just trying to make you laugh, you look a little tired."

"Well, I've been spending a lot of time working on a project. I'm not ready to talk about it yet, but I will in a couple of weeks. Peter's helping me out. I'd like you to stay away from his house for a few days. I have him swamped with work. He needs every second to help me. You'll see other people coming and going from his house. We hired some extra help. You might as well know—it appears Peter has a girlfriend. Her name is Ginger Mae. You'll meet her soon enough. She'll be running back and forth between the houses to keep me updated."

"Peter has a girlfriend? *That dog.* Do you like her?"

Abby wrinkled her nose at Scotty's question. "I'm not sure yet. But you'll like her, I can tell. She's the type that attracts men like flies on road kill."

"Meow." Scotty laughed. "What's the deal on this project? Why all the hush-hush?"

Abby stood and walked up to Scotty. Her face was deadly serious, inadvertently revealing a hint of fear. He felt a chill down his back.

"You have to trust me, hon, we'll all be okay, but this is urgently important."

Scotty glanced at Echo, who had stopped grooming Barney and was clearly listening. In a small voice he asked his last question. "Does this have anything to do with Echo or our changes?"

Abby did not answer. She turned to Echo, silent communication filling the room. She turned back to Scotty and squeezed his shoulders softly. "Yes."

Scotty's face blanched.

"Don't worry. We'll be okay," Abby repeated with emphasis.

He slowly finished with the dogs, saying nothing as he tried to absorb Abby's comments. Leaving them to their eating, he let himself out to the terrace, ambling down to the dock to find Kane as he tried to dispel his feeling of danger, weighing his concern over Abby's words. He knew his sister. She was scared. And if *she* was scared, well then so was he. Why hadn't Echo come to *him* with the problem? He wasn't sure if he should feel left out or not, realizing being a teenager had its limitations. He decided he had better pay a little more attention to things around the house. *Maybe Chloe will want to spend some time with me and the posse? She can bring her little monster, Teddy.*

Brightening, he approached the dock. He could see Captain Cobby busy with some mechanical thing, trying to un-jam it with a screwdriver.

"Hey, Captain. Kane around?"

"Yo, Scotty. He just went up to the carriage house to change. He found your note this morning but he had chores to finish first. He'll be ready in time. I'll send him up to the house by twelve. That okay?"

"Sure thing, Captain, thanks."

Captain Cobby stood up, coming toward Scotty at the end of the dock. "Thank you, Scotty, you're a good boy. Your mom would be proud."

Giving Captain Cobby a salute, Scotty headed back to the house to get his Jeep. Abby must have let the posse out because they were waiting for him on the terrace, tails rocking in syncopation.

"Come on, guys, back in the house. I have a day off today and you can't come." Laughing at their miserable faces, he snuck out to the garage, started the Jeep and headed to Chloe's house.

Arriving ten minutes later, he quickly found himself being led into her house by one of her father's men. Chloe was just coming down the stairs, Teddy in her arms and wrapped up in an old yellow and turquoise afghan.

"Do you mind if I bring Ted? It's so hard on him when I leave him behind. I thought I could leave him with your guys, now that they've already met." She grinned impishly, twirling around to show him her outfit.

"Yeah, sure, he'll be okay. I'll tell Echo to keep an eye on him."

"Echo again. I thought she was a cat."

Blushing, Scotty chastised himself for the casual slip.

"Yeah, but um, she'll still do a good job." He covered badly. Fortunately, his butt was saved by Mrs. Elbarad bustling into the foyer. She placed a jacket over Chloe, removing Teddy from her arms.

"No, no, Mrs. E., Ted's going with us." She scooped up the tiny handful, Teddy's pink tongue dancing over her face like a frantic butterfly. "Shall we go?" Scotty watched her smile, noticing light dance in her brown eyes as she led the way to the Jeep.

When they got to the house, Abby and Kane were waiting. They deposited Teddy in the house with his afghan, exchanged greetings and off they went.

*

The Big Cat Sanctuary sprawled out on the inland side of Sarasota where the land had managed to escape overdevelopment, housing a touch of old Florida. Mixed zoning, ramshackle hovels and quaint cottages led to the entrance to the sanctuary, which was well lit and off the main road.

Driving through the main gate, they bumped along a long dusty gravel driveway, parking in a mowed grassy field among the dozens of vehicles already there. Strolling into a small building where their entrance fee was collected by smiling volunteers, Scotty noticed most of them were clearly retired and occupying their time by honoring a passion for wildlife with their dedication to the sanctuary.

Abby got busy snapping photos. She took pictures of the entrance off the main road, the parking lot and the outbuildings. Scotty watched her back up to get long-distance shots of the enclosures. *What's up with her?* he wondered, as Chloe and Kane comfortably chatted each other up with Mrs. Elbarad trailing behind.

He must admit the animals grabbed him. The sanctuary housed over twenty bears from all parts of the world. There's nothing more awe inspiring than standing four feet in front of a six-hundred-pound brown bear resting on the side of his haunches, casually washing his face with a paw which could break your neck with one swipe, while he nodded amiably at the people gawking at him.

They observed primates with inquisitive tiny wise-man faces, a huge male tortoise ponderously chasing a lady tortoise, hoping to get her to hold still long enough to make new baby tortoises. They watched massive camels, tiny ponies, large exotic South American birds which made outrageous sounds, preening and performing for the crowds, and even a kangaroo. They got to touch a darling ring-tailed lemur, a precious mammal found only on the Island of Madagascar off the coast of Africa, its mighty tail a stunning and fluffy adornment any woman would kill for. And goats. Dozens of the petite ungulates with beautiful markings, tripping over themselves to stick out their tongues at the crowd, begging for the goodies sold for a few dollars to feed them. And a young discarded chimpanzee rescued by the sanctuary, his childlike human antics delighting the crowd.

Did you know that man had eaten chimps into extinction in Africa by 2030? Did you know monkeys had the tops of their skulls sawed off while alive, then positioned under dining tables which had holes cut out of the middle and were draped discreetly so that rich Asian businessmen would not have to watch the death spasms of the human-like primate as they spooned his live brain into their mouths?

Did you hear the story of the Asian restaurant owner who let his son play on the kitchen floor with a sun bear cub while he heated the water he was going to boil the cub in before serving it to rich diners in another room?

Did you know that, in Thailand, farmers chained bears up in boxes so small they could not move at any time in their whole lives while the farmers, without anesthesia, hooked their gall bladders up to archaic machines which would become part of them until they died of infections, pain or malnutrition, just so that the farmers could milk their gall bladders for fluid sold in illegal markets, the supposed antidote to male infertility?

Did you know the black bear had been hunted by men anxious to prove they had the biggest penis in the woods, for mere sport and trophies, all over the U.S. until they risked extinction by 2040?

Did you know elephants, rhinos and the glorious pièce de résistance, the Bengal tiger, had been slaughtered into extinction to make profit from selling their body parts by 2030?

And the most intelligent, creative, discerning man of the forest, the orangutan, like the chimpanzee and so many other primates, was extinct by 2025 through the destruction and theft of their homes for profit in Sumatra and Borneo. Did I mention men thought they tasted like chicken?

Do I even need to tell you what man has done to other wildlife species in all corners of the world?

Scotty finished reading the flyer handed to him by a young girl wearing a shirt that said *Please don't eat my friends*. A photo of her with an assortment of animals, cuddled protectively to her side, featured prominently on her shirt. He noted a little dog which looked unmistakably like Teddy. Shaking his head, he remembered he heard somewhere that people ate dogs and cats as delicacies. *Delicacies.* That meant they had other food. They viewed canines and felines as luxuries. *Yeah,* he thought bitterly, *men must have their luxuries.*

Disturbed, he tried to erase the abhorrent images from his mind. Looking around, he spied the group and caught up as they approached the tigers and lions. The first tigers he laid his eyes on were the mutant recessive gene white, and the awesome rich and velvety orange Siberian and Bengal. They were kept in a tiger version of giant dog runs. Chain-link fences kept them from escaping. At the back of the runs, they enjoyed access to a huge outdoor compound, complete with colossal boulders, trees and a pool of water.

Scotty approached the run of the most resplendent of the Siberians as he paced, calmly and deliberately, looming large. Very large: his paws massive, his head enormous. Scotty noticed his perfection marred by a missing piece of his left ear, near the tip. It looked like a perfect semi-circle. While Scotty admired the tiger, it approached. Standing in front of Scotty, he sat, adjusting his haunches comfortably, not taking his golden eyes off him. The tiger raised his paw to the chain-link fence, his needle-pointed claws hooking on the metal. Scotty stood inches away. He could actually reach out and touch the tiger if he was stupid enough. The organic sweet smell of the beast engulfed him as he inched closer. He could see the rhythmic rise and fall of the brilliant orange chest, its black velvet stripes moving in time. In that moment, he met the hypnotic stare of the magnificent beast. Neither moved; the tiger a statue.

The tiger suddenly shook his head as if to ward off an annoying fly, never taking his eyes off Scotty. Its eyes narrowed then widened, as if with some kind of recognition. In the pit of his stomach, Scotty felt a great injection of warmth working its way to his head. The space between the two of them slowly morphed. He found himself rising, looking down on the tiger as the fur dropped from the hide of the animal. Roaring deafeningly, the iconic cat fell to the floor, flesh melting to expose the great rib cage. Within seconds, the only signs of the precious magnificence that had stood before him were dissected bones, crumbling to dust. Scotty looked down the runs to the other cats. The runs were empty, only lonely piles of pulverized calcium remained. Scotty felt himself start to sweat. He reached up to wipe his forehead, feeling his hot clammy fingers wipe away the acrid evidence of what must be a delusional reaction.

Looking for his sister and friends, he found himself to be alone. He ran out of the kennel, shouting for them. The roaring silence thundered in his unhearing ears. No staff, no crowds, no Abby. He looked to the sky, shrinking back against the wall of another enclosure as he examined the sudden darkness, the sky preparing to snow. He felt a drop of moisture on his nose. Raising his hand, he caught a flake that drifted leisurely to land on his hand, the color of sludge, unusually large. The moisture from the flake burned his skin with its freezing incalescence. He felt crushed by an overwhelming premonition of despair and hopelessness. His breathing became labored as he fought for air. Gasping, he fell to the ground, his surroundings sluggishly closing in on him. The last thing he remembered was an image of Echo, flashing auras to his mind as he gradually toppled over onto his back, sinking into oblivion.

Chapter 9

"Dude, you okay?" The voice sounded familiar, but the face was indistinct. He fought the miasma that wanted to pull him back to oblivion. The face crystallized, revealing Kane's amused mug. "Are you sure you don't want to take off your windbreaker? You must be awful hot? With all that fur and all."

My fur? How did he know? Scotty's heart started a steady hammering as concern over Kane's question caught him off guard. He could make out Abby's voice in the background shooing Kane away. He heard the sound of a distant lawnmower and Chloe's voice pleading with the dogs to hush. *Sounds like Teddy took over the posse.* He realized his mind must be clearing. He struggled to sit up, wondering why he was home.

Abby knelt near his head, whispering, "You okay, hon? You gave me a scare there. I had the damnedest time getting you out of there. Someone called an ambulance. I couldn't let them examine you. Thank God, Kane knew what to do. I didn't realize you had told him about us. He stalled everyone while Chloe and I got you to the car. Do you remember anything?"

Scotty stood. He felt fine except for a lingering feeling of anxiety. *Kane covered for me?* "Can we talk about this later, Abby? I need to clear my head, that tiger's behavior unnerved me. I'll be fine. I want to get Chloe home and then we have to talk, okay?" Scotty spoke in a sober whisper, noticing Chloe's intense focus on them. He watched as Abby walked over to Kane. Placing her arm around his shoulders, she solemnly asked if he and his father would be available for a meeting later this evening. Kane smiled, his face reflecting wonder and respect.

"Sure, Abby, how late do you want us?" His voice was soft, all traces of the youthful wise guy gone at the tone of her seriousness.

"Nine should be fine. Call me if you have any changes. Tell your dad I look forward to seeing him." Smiling, she showed Kane out to the terrace.

"Okay, young lady, it's time for young Scott to take us home." Mrs. Elbarad stood impatiently, heading toward the front door. "Scott, are you sure you should drive? Perhaps your sister should take us home. I cannot have Miss Chloe in any jeopardy." Not getting any response, she bristled. "I am afraid I must insist."

"Okay. Ab, do you mind? I'll sit in the back with Chloe and Teddy. If we can get him in the car, that is." Teddy tried to elude Chloe's grip, running back to where Penny relaxed on her doggie bed, apparently oblivious to Teddy as he persistently climbed her back and straddled her neck in his ridiculous attempts to impregnate her floppy ear.

Driving to Chloe's house gave Scotty a chance to talk to her softly in the back seat. He was aware of Mrs. Elbarad's responsibilities, but resented her attention on any conversation he had with Chloe.

"I'm so sorry this turned out so badly. Do you think you might want to get together again?"

Chloe turned to him, her face brightening with pleasure. Teddy nestled exhausted in her lap on his afghan. "Yes, of course. I'm pretty free for the next few weeks. I just have my morning swim sessions with my coach. Practice starts with the team in June, so I have to be ready to prequalify my time. Why don't you come over tomorrow for lunch? We can hang out at the pool. Bring your suit."

Scotty grimaced. The last thing he wanted to do was deal with Chloe questioning why he wouldn't take off his shirt. Sensing his discomfort she punched him lightly in the arm.

"Okay, I get it, we'd better do something less strenuous until we find out what happened to you today. We can hang out with the monkeys. Want to bring any of the dogs? Ted could sure use the company. Although I have yet to meet your elusive cat, Echo. Where are you hiding her?"

"Monkeys sound great. And Echo was probably hiding in one of the bedrooms." He patted her hand and gave her a return punch on the arm. "I'm hoping you'll get to meet Echo sometime soon. She really is special."

"What could be so special about a cat?"

Scotty looked closely into Chloe's face. He fought the urge to count the freckles liberally sprinkled across her nose, a casualty of the hot Sarasota sun. He looked for a sign, something that would show him that his secret would be safe with her. Regretfully, he decided he didn't know her well enough. Yet.

"She's special, you'll see. In good time." They grinned at each other, two young kids just happy to have discovered they really liked each other.

Driving back home, Abby announced she was going to run over to Peter's for a few minutes. She suggested he walk the dogs then go take a nap. She would be back in about an hour, then they could talk. She also wanted him available for her meeting tonight with the Cobbys. Scotty nodded, his mind elsewhere. Saying goodbye, he rounded up the posse to take them out to the terrace.

Echo had decided it was safe to show her face and latched on to Mimi to the consternation of Barney. The extra attention Echo devoted to Mimi had helped her to integrate more fully into the posse. Her food aggressions diminished as she gained confidence. Her demeanor had brightened. She no longer wandered around the house like the ugly new girl, and was well on her way to becoming a well-balanced happy doggy.

Scotty watched her frolic on the terrace, wishing it could be so easy for him. He no longer showed any signs of his infirmities, but he felt like they still owned part of him. He reflected on the improvement in Kane's behavior toward him. That was a blessing.

He would make a better attempt to get to know him, try to include him more often. Maybe he might end up with a friend after all. He was tempted to think things were looking up; if only he could shake his heavy case of the heebie-jeebies.

He made himself comfortable on the wicker lounge chair, stretching out to soak up the sun that had decided to show up after all. That usually made him feel better. Closing his eyes, he thought about Chloe and wondered how long it would take before she asked him about the ever-present sunglasses. He had noticed more than one curious glance at them. *Bound to happen soon.* Breathing deeply, he nodded off.

Ginger Mae answered the front door, not surprised to find Abby standing there, impatience plastered on her face.

"Come in, Abby, things are a little crazy here, but Peter says he's making progress." She ran her hands through her blond hair, straightening her skirt that crept up her thighs when unaware. She hadn't expected Abby or she would have changed. Most of the staff who showed up to work were men. Her philosophy was to always dress for the boys; you never knew when you might need them, or their money for that matter. A girl must be prepared to take care of herself at all times. And that often meant looking ahead to the next male opportunity around the corner.

Ginger Mae scampered quickly to catch up with Abby as she strolled without stopping to chat. *Figures,* she thought venomously. Abby always made her feel like the hired help. As they approached Peter's office they could hear murmurings through the door. Abby opened the door before Ginger Mae could reach for it.

"Will you excuse us, please?" Abby looked archly at Ginger Mae, closing the door in her face. Ginger Mae steamed. *What's all the secrecy about?* Peter would not let her in his office when he spoke on the phone, appearing vague when she asked questions. She knew it had something to do with hiring truckers for something. Her job consisted of editing the list of potential drivers and researching their police records on Peter's Lexus-Nexus program. A second group of drivers had to answer some very personal questions about their families and their pets. All potential candidates were funneled to Peter for salary negotiations and the specifics of what they would be hauling. That seemed to be the big secret. She put her ear to the door, hearing nothing. Miffed, she decided to go check on Daisy. She wanted to dress her up and bring her down to meet Abby. Maybe that would help the golden holier-than-thou ice queen melt.

Knocking on Daisy's bedroom door, the little girl came running. She threw her arms around Ginger Mae's legs, burying her bony dark-brown head in them. Ginger Mae untangled the child and lifted her up with Daisy wrapping her legs around Ginger Mae's waist.

"Hey, Daisy Chain. What's my girl doing?" Daisy looked up brightly, pointing to her storybooks spread on the floor. She might not speak, but Ginger had taught her to read and do numbers, something she had picked up at an early age. She now read on what Ginger Mae estimated to be a fifth-grade level. She had learned to add and subtract complex numbers over a year ago; single digits bored her. According to her age she should be ready for kindergarten. Ginger hadn't thought it necessary to enroll her yet, as she excelled far past anything she could learn in that kind of class. Crossing her fingers, she hoped to settle down here and find a more advanced placement for the child. Her child. Brushing Daisy's fine hair out of her face, she reminded herself that Daisy belonged to her, not her nonexistent brother. Sometimes she had trouble separating her own lies from reality.

"Daisy, I want you to wash your face and put on your Sunday dress with your white shoes. Hurry now," she said, leading the child into her bathroom. "I have someone special I want you to meet. We need to impress her, so put on your biggest smile."

Mother and daughter walked reverently down the art deco stairway to the foyer, where Daisy ran up to stroke the huge ornamental cats standing guard against the wall. Ginger still praised God for the luck she had stumbled on when she met Peter: landing in such a fine home in such a prestigious location. Things were still going well between them, but she did encounter trouble in claiming her share of his attention with Miss Ice Queen making him dance for her. Desperate to bring this relationship along, she needed to cultivate a deeper intimacy quickly, in case of catastrophe: Armoni finding out where she lived. Taking a chair near Peter's office, she boosted Daisy up on her lap to wait.

It took thirty minutes for his door to open. Daisy kicked off one of her shoes, trying to shove the other one down the front of her pinafore, sideways. At the click of the opening door, Ginger Mae jumped up, dumping Daisy on the floor with a thud. Scrambling, Ginger Mae bent over to help her daughter up, her skirt hiking itself to a dangerous level.

"And who do we have here?" It was Abby, coolly surveying the melee. Breathlessly, Ginger introduced her daughter as her niece.

"Well, I need to get back to work," Peter interrupted, mumbling a goodbye and returning to his office. *Thanks a lot,* Ginger Mae thought indignantly. *I have to be left alone with the ice queen?* She shook off her exasperation, suddenly realizing the atmosphere strummed with silence. Turning from Peter's door, she saw Daisy frozen, looking directly at Abby. Abby stood silently, just staring at the child. *What's going on?* Ginger Mae nervously wondered as she stared at Abby's back. *Why doesn't Abby say something?*

From where Ginger Mae stood, she could clearly observe Daisy's face. The child had many expressions, her way of communicating with those in her limited world. But Ginger Mae didn't recognize this one. She watched as Abby raised her hand to her face. It returned to her side, clutching the ever-present sunglasses. She approached Daisy, who watched spellbound, her face a cipher. Ginger Mae moved forward, only to be cut off by Abby's hand held commandingly in the air, her back still to Ginger Mae. Abby's voice came clearly and casually from in front of her without turning her head.

"Ginger Mae, would you be kind enough to fetch me a glass of water?" Ginger Mae frowned, thinking she had heard Abby wrong. "Water?"

Abby nodded without turning.

"Certainly, right away." Ginger beat herself up, all the way to the kitchen. *Why do I lose it around Abby? I might as well get down on the floor and clean her shoes. I need to get a backbone, especially since I'm older than she is. I should be the one giving the orders— this is Peter's house and I am Peter's girlfriend.* Returning with the water, she saw Abby sitting on one of the chairs, her sunglasses in place, with Daisy at her feet.

"Come on, sweetie, the nice lady doesn't want to see you sitting on the floor."

"That's okay, Mommy, Abby doesn't mind."

The glass of water slipped from Ginger Mae's hand and crashed to the floor, forgotten, as she started to shake, tears flowing soundlessly from her eyes. She whispered, stunned, "Daisy?"

Smiling as if nothing was amiss, Daisy stood. She went to Abby and picked up her hand. Ginger was sure some kind of silent communication was going on. She sniffed the air, noticing a smell she couldn't identify.

"Baby, come here." Daisy put Abby's hand down and ran to Ginger Mae, throwing her arm around her neck as her mother picked her up. She turned to face Abby.

"Well," Abby said kindly, "I guess I'll leave you two ladies alone now."

"Will I see you again, Abby?" Daisy sounded anxious.

"Yes, my dear, we're going to be great friends." Smiling, Abby turned to leave the room without a word to the stunned Ginger Mae.

Abby returned to her own house, grateful that Peter was taking his new task seriously. He had made great progress, apparently finding it not as difficult as she feared it would be to locate truckers willing to do the job. For the right money, of course. An unexpected surprise pleased her to no end. A large number of the truckers were women. A wonderful stroke of luck. *Echo will be very happy when I report the news. That will make things easier in the long run.*

But the most amazing turn was meeting Daisy. Abby knew instinctively she would become very important to her; to the mission. She didn't know how or why but she knew it was worth the risk to cure her. Examining her surprising reaction to the child, Abby felt forlorn. *What an odd reaction. Where did that come from?* she wondered. Shaking her head, she pushed the mystery aside to consider Daisy. Of course, that now meant she would have to add the questionable Ginger Mae to her plans. She had always planned to include Peter, so it should be no problem. She hoped Jose would understand. She missed having him home, but understood he must resolve the problems with the rest of his missing family. And she certainly wanted them to be safe. She just hoped he would hurry home so she didn't have to make a change of plans regarding Mama Diaz and the girls. Now it was time to do some explaining to Scotty and prepare for the Cobbys.

Entering the kitchen, she noticed Scotty asleep on the terrace. She stepped outside to call in the dogs. Echo followed, riding on Barney's back with Mimi scampering alongside, trying in vain to jump up on Barney to join Echo. Scotty woke up, stretched, and joined her in the kitchen, taking a comfortable seat at the table, his elbows on the marble top. She noted his hands had a slight tremor. Seating herself next to him, she covered his hands with her own, a gesture that usually reassured him.

"You know, don't you?" She faced him directly as he bowed his head.

"I don't know much, Ab, but I think something is going to happen. Something bad, something scary." He looked up, his face suddenly exposing a hint of the man he would become. "I think we are part of it somehow, aren't we? At the sanctuary, I felt like I was being sent some kind of a message. The tiger. He meant something to me. I could feel him. Do you know about any of this?"

Echo climbed up onto the table, her face expressionless. Abby felt the aura in her mind as Echo spoke to Scotty. "It is almost time, Brother. We are preparing. You will have a part as time draws near. The mission has changed. We can only save a few, as time grows short."

"Abby, what's going to happen?" He read the guilty expression on her face. "You know, don't you? Echo, why have you hidden this from me? Don't I have a right to know?" His fist pounded on the marble; frustration, sorrow and confusion fighting their way across the planes of his suddenly colorless face. "It's not fair. How much more can we take?"

"We will all prevail, Brother Scotty. I have chosen my Brothers and my Sister well. I waited for over a century." Echo withdrew, scrambling off the table to join Barney, letting Barney rest his head on her tiny lap while Mimi tried to insert herself between the two of them. Penny slumbered, oblivious as usual.

"Scotty, I only learned of it a few days ago. I too received a message. You through a tiger, me, a woman or a spirit. I'm not sure what she was. She looked a lot like us, though. Her body showed changes, only more developed. She showed me what must be done. But I don't know what's going to happen. Only a rough idea of when. We must collect these animals and go back home."

"What? Are you crazy? I'm not going back home. I'm just starting to have a life here." He stood, dumping his chair over on its back. "Wait, are we being given any choice here?"

"No, we have no choice. If we stay here, we'll die. I think you know we have to do this. Try to be strong, Scotty. We'll learn more when the time comes. But I need your help now. In a few minutes, Kane and his father will be here. They'll be instrumental to us. It's going to be difficult, but I think I might need to reveal ourselves to get their cooperation. They need to go with us. I don't think I can do this without them."

"Can't Echo just wave her tail or speak to the Womb and make everything better?" Scotty sounded like he was going to cry.

"No, hon, I don't think that is what everything is all about. It's bigger and deeper. And way out of Echo's control."

They startled, hearing a tap on the French doors. Scotty rose to let Kane and his father in. Captain Cobby pulled up a chair, looking from Abby to Scotty, seeing their long faces. "Who died?"

The tension in the room tightened. Abby rose, saying nothing. Matter-of-factly, she went to the ornate walnut sideboard which dominated the kitchen. She returned to the table with a bottle of brandy. "Scotty, can you please get me the glasses?"

Returning with the snifters, Scotty watched Abby pour them all a generous shot. Kane looked between their faces. "Are we celebrating something?"

Abby could see the confusion and tentative smiles on their faces. She just did not know how to tell them. The silence lengthened. She could see a slow dawning on Captain Cobby's face, as he sensed the serious intent behind her invitation. She started slowly.

"I need you both to know you have been a great help to us in the short time we've lived here."

"We're getting fired," Kane blurted. His father put his hand on his arm, quieting him. Abby smiled, the tension released.

"No, of course not. You are almost part of our family now. I asked you to come over because I need your help with something deadly serious." Abby's voice strengthened with resolve. She spoke slowly and quietly. "I know I can trust you both, but I must have your oath that this will remain between us. If you decide you can't help me, so be it. But I am confident you will see things my way."

"Well, you sound very mysterious. You have our word. Why don't you just come out and ask us?" Captain Cobby motioned his head upward, a sign of encouragement.

"Okay. In about two weeks, I'm having some trucks here to deliver wildlife that I hope to load onto the yacht and have you deliver to Tampa. I will have a private jet on standby at the airport to fly us all to Newark Airport where we will join another convoy. The two of you, along with Scotty, Peter and his girlfriend, her niece and the dogs will go on to Sussex where Jose and I will join you later. The animals will be offloaded and you will take them to safety with you. Scotty will show you where. I am inviting you to stay with us." Abby looked at three blank faces, realization suddenly dawning on Scotty's face. He opened his mouth to say something but snapped it shut, saying nothing.

"Wow, that sounds like a pretty big job. Just what kind of animals are we talking?"

"I'm not going to lie to you. They'll be big. Lots of cats, some camels, goats, some bears, some smaller wildlife." Her voice tapered off as she saw the expressions on their faces.

"Are you kidding me? We can't fit cages for those kinds of animals on the boat. We don't have that kind of room. And where exactly are you getting them from?" Kane's eyes suddenly lit up as he glanced at Scotty.

"Does this have anything to do with what happened at the cat sanctuary today?"

Abby and Scotty were silent. The captain's eyes narrowed, suspicion doing a slow bloom on his face. As she expected it would.

"I don't understand why you want us to live with you in your old town, we live here. I don't want to move. My friends are here, our life is here." Kane looked incredulous.

"Abby, you aren't stealing these animals are you?" Captain Cobby's voice remained low and calm.

"Yes. Yes, I am," she said succinctly.

"But why? Why would you want to do that?" Shaking his handsome head disbelievingly, Captain Cobby took a sip of his brandy. "This does not sound like the Abby I thought I knew."

Sighing deeply, Abby knew the time had come. She pointed over to the dogs. "Do you see Echo over there? I'm sorry but we had to lie to you. Our father was not a famous scientist. He was a no-good bastard who left us when Scotty was seven. Echo is a fully functioning natural creature. She can do many wondrous things. Such as heal. As a child I contracted a life-threatening illness. She cured me. As a result, I was given certain powers and certain responsibilities. The animals are part of the responsibilities. Something horrible is going to happen. Millions will be killed. It's part of Echo's assignment to do this. If you come with us you'll be safe from the threat."

Abby saw that she wasn't getting through to them. Kane had a look of embarrassment on his face. His father was laughing.

"Echo's assignment? Abby, you sure know how to tell a good one. You had me going for a while." The captain slapped his knee and punched Kane in the arm. "What do you think of that, boy?" Kane looked around uncertainly.

Abby slowly rose. She took off her sunglasses, the golden rainbow swirls from her eyes lighting up the room. At their shocked faces, she raised her hands over her head, stripping off her shirt, exposing her fine golden fur, just like Echo. Without turning, she shook out her wings which had grown to almost adult size. They were dumbstruck, flickers of fear in their eyes. She nodded to Scotty. He rose. With an audible deep breath, he dropped his glasses and removed his shirt.

"Holy shit!"

No one said another word. Abby just let them look and absorb. They stared at Echo as if seeing her for the first time. They downed their brandy. Abby forced herself not to speak. Instead, she picked up the bottle, calmly refilling everyone's glasses. She folded her wings against her body, replaced her shirt and sat down. The mundane gesture seemed to calm everyone down. Scotty remained standing as if ready to take flight. Abby reached out and pulled him down into his seat. No one spoke.

The silence hung in the air like a rubber balloon, stretched beyond its limits, ready to rupture. For some reason, Mimi chose this moment to waddle over to the table and scratch on Scotty's chair, her little half-blind bug eyes demanding attention. Scotty bent down to pick her up. He set her on his lap so she could sit up and see everyone. He kissed her tenderly on her head. The tension broke.

"*I knew it.* I knew there was something odd about you. I caught a glimpse of your ah, your unusualness the other night when you took a swim with the dogs." Kane looked pleased to have his suspicions confirmed.

Abby couldn't resist asking. "Why didn't you mention it to anyone? You kept his secret?"

"Yeah, dude, you covered for me."

Kane's face turned red, his shoulders trying to shrug off the moment. "It's nothing."

"Do you think you might put your glasses back on, guys? I seem to be having some trouble concentrating while I look at you."

They did as the captain asked. "Well," he continued, stopping to clear his throat. He paused, taking another gulp of the brandy. "I have a million questions that, I guess, can wait. But I think this calls for us to talk about how we are going to be able to fit all this wildlife on the boat."

Abby broke out in a torrent of tears. She jumped up from her seat to run to Captain Cobby. He stood and grabbed her in a bear hug. She sobbed all over his shirt, breaking down about how hard it had been for them, how lonely, they couldn't make friends, she missed her mother, how scared she always was. Captain Cobby held her until she slowed down, stroking her thick hair and telling her it would be okay. They were there for her. Looking into his competent reassuring face, she knew they had a chance now.

Chapter 10

Ginger Mae swam in Peter's jazzy heated pool, built in the shape of a sea gull with its wings wide open. She tried to convince Daisy to join her in the water at the shallow end. But Daisy was afraid of the water.

"No, Mommy, I'm not ready yet. I need to work up more nerve, besides Peter gave me these books about vampires. I want to read them. I'm going to sit in the shade and read Dracula. It's very old. You stay in and enjoy yourself." Daisy sounded adorable. Adult conversation in a tiny little-girl voice.

"Okay, Daisy Chain. Let me know if you decide to go inside." Ginger Mae swam to the other end of the pool, looking tanned and fit, thanks to her daily swims. It had been almost two weeks since Daisy had started to talk. Ginger Mae was amazed every time she opened her mouth. She could now see she had greatly underestimated her daughter. Her IQ must be much higher than she had realized. She had shocked them both when they found her trying to climb the shelves in Peter's library to reach one of Peter's old college textbooks—on physics, no less. Peter hadn't seemed particularly impressed when he learned Daisy could speak. Of course he'd only known her for two days at the time. He didn't seem to understand these words were the first she had ever spoken.

Things were starting to progress nicely. Their project seemed pretty much complete, except for the pickup, whatever that meant. Peter had started to take an interest in Daisy's education since he had learned she was a prodigy. The two of them were becoming great buddies. *That's half the battle.* As soon as they completed the pickup on Abby's project, they were going to shop for a school for Daisy.

Her personal relationship with Peter still proceeded slowly. The sex was alright, it wasn't that. But he treated her like a delicate flower. It could be downright annoying sometimes. It made it hard to really bond with him. She wasn't a delicate flower. And until he realized it, they would never develop the kind of relationship that would stand the stress of obstacles that might come their way. Like Armoni. She was dying to confess some of her history to him so he wouldn't go into shock at the wrong time—when she needed him to be strong. She had dropped a few oblique hints, but he hadn't picked up on them. She still couldn't believe she had slipped away from Armoni so easily. Perhaps her past prevented her from fully bonding with Peter, fully convinced the shoe would drop sooner or later.

In the meantime, she tried to be as indispensable as possible. She had learned never to say no to anything Peter asked of her. She knew all the names of the truckers and their histories. She was an excellent messenger as she made her way between the homes several times a day. Her relationship with Abby, if you could call it that, thawed about 10 percent. But that did count as an improvement. *I will wear that bitch down sooner or later, even if I have to use Daisy to do it.*

Clearly, Abby harbored some sort of interest in Daisy. She had discovered Daisy huddled with Abby in her study one day. She hadn't even known Daisy had left the house. She wondered how Daisy even knew where to find Abby. She was only five years old, after all.

One day, while Ginger Mae gave her report to Abby, Daisy wandered out of the study. Ginger Mae found her in the kitchen with the dogs. She could see Scotty, Abby's brother, outside on the terrace with his girlfriend, Chloe. The girl seemed to be with Scotty all the time. Cute couple but Chloe seemed a bit young.

The most amazing thing happened while she tried to round up Daisy from the kitchen. In walked this funny little creature. She would have thought it was a cat or a monkey, except for the odd long lion tail, or the shining—*was that glass?*—antlers and what looked like deformed or broken leather wings sprouting from its back. And the creature's eyes, something was definitely wrong with the poor thing, it must be sick. Grabbing Daisy, she tried to drag her away.

"No, Mommy, I want to stay here. Please don't call my friend an *it*. I love her. Echo, tell my mommy we're friends."

The creature just stood silently, her eyes giving Ginger Mae a stomachache.

Ginger Mae wondered if Echo might be the *scumbag mother fuckin' freaky pet* that Armoni had always complained about. The one he had said he wanted to stomp.

Suspicion shrouded her every waking moment as she realized something very odd occupied Peter and Abby at that house. She had accepted Daisy's sudden speech appearance as a coincidence. If she hadn't been in the kitchen getting water for Abby, Ginger Mae would have been with her daughter when it happened. *Interesting—Abby suddenly needing a drink of water. Maybe that was to get me out of the room. But for what purpose?* Peter had let slip that Abby and Scotty were filthy rich, but he wouldn't tell her why. Father deserted, mother recently deceased. She heard talk of Abby's boyfriend, Jose, yet she never saw him around. She wondered if he wore the constant sunglasses too. Peter said they had a genetic infection thing— couldn't tolerate light. If anyone needed sunglasses, it was that sick little creature in the kitchen.

"Mommy, I'm going back in the house."

Ginger Mae swam back to Daisy's end of the pool. She watched her daughter rise from her lounge chair and put on her little robe. Her heart swelled with pride. *How did I ever produce such a wonder?*

"Okay, baby." She boosted herself up and out of the pool, not bothering with the stairs. "I'm just going to lie in the sun for a few more minutes. If you see Peter, tell him I'll be starting dinner in an hour. Pork chops, okay?"

Nodding and kissing her mother, Daisy trotted off, book in hand. Ginger Mae settled in, comfortable in her lounge chair, the sun sending a sleepy languid sultriness into her body. *Umm*, she thought,

I might just have to seduce Peter before dinner. A smile spread itself sexily across her face.

A hand from nowhere slapped itself down on her mouth. A voice from hell asked, "Got any of those pork chops for me, you two-timin' thievin' cunt?"

Scotty walked down to the beach within eyeshot of Chloe's father's mansion. He waved goodbye to Kane as he headed back to the boat to help with the modifications needed for the animals. It hadn't been easy keeping his horrible secret from Chloe. They had spent time together almost every day since the excursion to the cat sanctuary. Sometimes Kane joined them when he wasn't needed by his father. The three of them had developed an infectious camaraderie which helped sustain Scotty and Kane as their mission approached. Then he thought of Chloe. When he was with her, he sometimes forgot what a freak he had become. When they laughed at the same silly things, he almost felt like his life could be normal. Today was Chloe's birthday. She would be sixteen.

Today, her father planned a big party for her at a swank hotel downtown. He hoped he hadn't damaged Chloe's feelings too much when he'd declined to come. He understood her anxiousness for him to meet her father and he felt flattered, but Abby just would not let him risk exposure. He got it. The last thing he wanted was to be the object of ridicule in front of a bunch of giggling teenage girls that he didn't know. Kane would attend, though, and had agreed to help Scotty pass Chloe a note, asking her to meet him on the beach near her house, after her party.

The party had ended two hours ago and he still waited.

Kane joined him on the beach to report on the celebrations. He admitted his own discomfort—swank parties were not his scene. He mentioned Chloe's agitation, aggravated by the presence of a gorgeous woman at her father's side. It seemed her father had himself a girlfriend. It had certainly taken the attention off Chloe. Scotty knew she would be bummed out by that. She complained over and over about not getting enough time with her father as it was. She was really psyched to have him at her party. Scotty thought her father sounded like an insensitive ass, just like his own father. Just because her father didn't beat her or humiliate her didn't mean she didn't feel the damage.

The sun made its inevitable slide under the horizon. He glanced at his watch, aware of the lateness of the hour, knowing he needed to go home. Tomorrow stood to be a stressful day. He felt excited and scared—and very sad. He planned to say goodbye to Chloe after he gave her his special birthday present, one of the few things he owned that held any meaning. He raised his head. In the distance he could hear the sound of a soft lawnmower. Rising to his feet he spotted her running toward him down the beach, rascally Teddy at her heels. She arrived breathlessly.

"Hi, sorry I'm so late," she gasped, trying to catch her breath. "The darn reporters. They just wouldn't let us alone. My father had some doll face with him. It might have been nice if he'd have warned me about her before my birthday. Reporters crashed the party and took over." She sighed, throwing back her head and scrunching her eyes shut. "Thanks, Dad, swell party. It's bad enough my mom couldn't be there, but I guess he's already replaced her." Her bitterness threatened to overwhelm the special moment Scotty had long anticipated.

"Hey, babe, it's your night now. Just the two of us. Isn't that what you want?"

"*Yes.* Let's forget about everyone else. Just us—oh, and Ted." She bent down to pick him up and gave him a little toss in the air, catching him and hugging him to her chest. "He's my guy."

"And I thought I was the one."

Throwing her hands around his neck, she demanded impishly. "So, where's my birthday kiss?" Scotty laughed at her irrepressible nature. She never stayed down for long. He felt like a man dying of gloom who had just found a cocktail of sunshine. She helped him forget.

Pulling her down on the sand, he gave her a quick peck on her cheek.

"Are you kidding me? Come here, you." She swept Teddy away and stood on her knees, wrapping her arms around his neck. "I know you can do better than that."

Laughing, tired of teasing her, he showed her that he could, planting a long slow one on her lips. After they stopped rolling around in the sand, he picked up his gift for her.

"I have a birthday present for you."

She smiled, her eyes alight with the excitement of first love.

"I see you do."

"I want you to know that this is one of the oldest things I own. It's very special to me. It gave hope to me and my mother for a long time, back when we were poor. And it was a big part of my childhood. I hope you will think of me whenever you wear it."

Chloe's face looked somber as she took the small package, unwrapping it to expose a black velvet jewelry box. She glanced quizzically up at Scotty. Opening it up, nestled against the velvet, lay an old gold coin, mounted on a platinum and gold bezel. Scotty lifted it out of the box, unclasping the heavy platinum and gold chain that held the coin, placing it around Chloe's neck. "I hope you like it."

"Like it? You must be kidding. It's gorgeous. I love it. I love it because it was yours and you cared to give it to me." Looking down, she said, "You know I'm crazy about you."

He reached out his hand, tipping her face up to his. His lip softly met hers as his tears slid down his cheeks. He broke off, wiping them away.

"Scotty, what's wrong?"

He looked at her with eyes deeply filled with anguish. "I have to say goodbye, Chloe."

"What do you mean?" Her voice sounded tiny with confusion. "Are you saying we have to break up?"

"No. I would *never* want to do that. We're moving back home tomorrow."

"You gotta be kidding me. Why so sudden? Why did you wait so long to tell me?" She gripped his hand painfully. "*Tomorrow?* I just don't understand." She touched her necklace. Scotty stayed silent, lost for words. "Can we please talk about this, Scotty?"

"I can't change anything, Chloe. And I can't explain. You wouldn't understand."

"How do you know if you don't give me a chance?" Her voice screeched incredulously as he grabbed her head with both his hands, pulling her toward him. He held his lips to her forehead.

"You have to know how much this hurts, Chloe. Please try. Try to understand. I don't want to hurt you. I would do anything to prevent that. I wish you could come with me."

Chloe pushed him away, anger bubbling to the surface. "Don't be ridiculous, you know I can't come with you. What would my father say? You're not giving me anything to go on. What's the big secret?" She stared at Scotty, his face giving him away. "There *is* a secret, *isn't there*? Why can't you tell me? I tell you everything. Don't you trust me?"

Scotty clammed up, then: "I'm not like you, Chloe."

"What's that supposed to mean?"

"It means exactly what I said." He knew he sounded bitter. All the frustrations of the last few years suddenly overflowed, Scotty unable to hold back. "You want to know why? You want to know what the secret is. Just remember that I love you and never wanted to hurt you." His bitterness out of control, he whipped off his shades. In the darkness, his eyes dazzled. Teddy froze, then opined with his ear-splitting bark.

"Interesting. That's all you've got for me? Just your weird eye disease? Ted, please." She picked up Teddy and attempted to comfort him. "You've got to do better than that."

Scotty shook his head back and forth. "I appreciate your unimpressed attitude, but I don't think you want to know anymore."

Chloe suddenly set Teddy down. Her face showed her outrage. "Let me ask you a question, Scott Preston. And I want the truth. Does Kane know about this?"

"Yes," he whispered. She started to cry. "No, please don't cry. I was afraid to tell you. I thought it would scare you away. And now you hate me anyway."

"I don't hate you, you big dummy," she sniffled. "You trust Kane more than me. I feel like a fool. It's a little odd, but it's just a little disease, for Pete's sake."

"It's not a disease."

She looked up, wiping her eyes with the bottom of her shirt. "Well, what is it then?" Rising, he did the only thing he could to explain. He removed his shirt, flexed his tail and let his fully developed resplendent wings unfold from his body. She looked up with big eyes, her mouth wide open. Teddy had no problem voicing his opinion.

"*Oh-my-God.*" She backed up on the sand. "Are you an angel?"

Scotty flexed his wings, feeling how good it was to be free of his shirt. Furling them back against his body, he put his shirt back on. Replacing his shades, he sat morosely on the sand. He rubbed his hands over his face, stifling a sob.

"I'm not an angel, I don't know what I am anymore. I just want to be a normal guy like I used to be. Something bad is going to happen. We don't know what. But we have to leave to prepare for it. My sister wants to save the animals from the Big Cat Sanctuary. I do too. And then we're leaving. That's all I know." He sounded drained, even to himself. Quietly, he added, "You can come if you want. It would make me very happy if you did."

"Does Abby know you have wings?"

"Yes. She has them too. So does Jose."

He heard Chloe swallow.

"Can you fly?"

"I haven't tried. Not exactly discreet."

She nodded, agreeing. He thought she might be accepting it. Not that it mattered all that much, he was leaving after all. But it would be nice if they could part without her mad at him. "Are you still mad at me?"

"I guess not. I'm very sorry this happened to you. I wish you could stay. Maybe we could get to the bottom of this." She sounded hopeless.

He stood, drawing her into an embrace. He could tell she knew that wouldn't happen. He knew by her tears as they soaked into his shirt. The moon came out, illuminating the sand, shining brightly on the confused young sweethearts being torn apart by forces bigger than themselves.

Abby reviewed the details of the rescue from her study. They planned to start very early in the morning, hoping to catch everyone unawares, before the volunteers or tourists arrived. Peter had just left. He came alone to update her. Nothing much had changed, the update was unnecessary. Her curiosity piqued, she wondered why he had thought it was needed. Ginger Mae had always been the one to run messages since Abby preferred to have the information in person, not over the cell. You never knew who might be listening. Funny, Peter hadn't really said much of anything. So unlike him. The assignment must have taken a toll on him. Or could it be the effects of the implant? He looked bad. Tired and wrinkled. Just not himself.

She made a note to drop in on them tonight. Maybe it was time to reveal herself and remove the implant. Once they saw the urgency, she was sure they would fall into line, anxious to save themselves. And Daisy, of course. Daisy hadn't been over to see Abby in quite a while. Tapping her finger on her writing desk, she realized that was out of the ordinary too.

She glanced at her watch, anxious to call Jose, who had finally located Mama Diaz and the girls. He had been delayed while one of the girls finished participating in an event at school, proud she could show off to Jose. Inadvertently, the event had played into her plans, keeping them from getting underfoot while she planned the rescue.

Now the time had come to break the news to Jose. She couldn't afford to let him return home. She called the airline, cancelling their flights to Florida. Change of plans. She wanted Jose to take them back to the house on Lily Pond Road where they could wait safely. Dialing Jose's cell, she heard him pick up. Taking a deep breath she started to talk.

An hour later she turned off her cell. Jose had agreed to return to Lily Pond Road. They were willing to await her explanations when she herself arrived. Jose hadn't taken it well. Actually, he hit the roof. Somehow, she had convinced him of the urgency, concluding with the surprise that she planned to bring other people with her. That had really stumped him. Especially when she told him she had disclosed their condition to the Cobbys. That had rendered him speechless. Wasting no time, she had concluded their conversation with a quick, "I love you," and said goodbye, checking off one more worry.

Pausing to rub her back where her wings were aching, she wondered where she could find Echo. The enigmatic creature had become her greatest source of comfort these last few days. She didn't need to pretend with Echo but found moral support. Echo helped prop her shoulders up when they desperately wanted to sag. *Well, I can't put it off any longer. I better get the visit to Peter out of the way.*

Crossing between the two houses, she ducked under the palms. She stood on Peter's doorstep, ringing the doorbell. *Where is he?* She could see light and shadows moving through his leaded glass doors. She rang again. Finally, the door opened.

"Hi, I just dropped by to make sure we're ready to go."

Peter bounced back and forth between his feet like a child trying to hold his urine. "Go? Where we going?" He took her hand and pulled her into the room, shutting the door.

"Coffee? Is there something I can do for you?" Peter noisily dragged a Frank Lloyd Wright chair to the living room sofa, leaving obvious scratches in the imported Brazilian hardwood floor. Abby stared at the scratches.

"No, thank you." Abby frowned, taken aback at the formality of the question. They had talked about nothing but the rescue for weeks. *What's wrong with him?* Looking closer at Peter, she saw sweat beading on his forehead. His Oxford shirt showed damp sweat rings. An odor redolent of moldy wet hay clung to him. *Is he sick?* Peter did not appear to be listening. His focus seemed to be out the window, overlooking the lawn currently being mowed by Louis, their Latino groundskeeper, fully engrossed in gyrating his torso to the silent tunes on his earphones.

"*Peter!*" Reeling his attention back inside the room, he stared slack-mouthed at Abby.

"What's the matter with you?" Abby stood up, disappointment and concern in her voice. "If you're sick, call a doctor. Pull yourself together. Take a shower for God's sake and call me later."

"Now, now, Abby, don't be so hasty, I—"

"No, Peter, I'll see you later." Abby slammed the front door, letting her body language speak for her. She wondered if she had made a mistake about Peter. Her mind reeled with the implications. This was so unlike him. Was something wrong? Was this a result of Ginger Mae's effect on him? Or was it the implant? *I better go find Echo.*

Chapter 11

Peter followed Abby; his eyes bleary from the sidelights flanking the leaded-glass double doors. Holding his breath, he said a desperate prayer asking God to help him get out of this alive. From the kitchen, he heard the click of a gun being cocked. Exhaling, he turned around, knowing exactly what awaited him.

There Armoni stood on the black porcelain floor, perfectly at home wearing Peter's silk dressing gown; a knife he called 'Kelly's favorite baby' in one hand, a shiny new Austrian semi-automatic Glock in the other.

"You did good for a little faggot. Now get your swishy fag ass in here."

Peter hurried into the kitchen where Daisy and Ginger Mae sat strapped to chairs. Ginger Mae had taken the brunt of Armoni's psychotic anger. Her swollen face, turned black and blue, bore a deep knife slash from her forehead to her lip, which hung partially detached from her face. Crusted blood dripped from her neck to her waist. Since last night, no one had been allowed to sleep. The whole sordid story had come out about Ginger Mae and Armoni. He had held a knife to Daisy's throat while he forced Ginger Mae to recite to Peter every vile sexual act she had done for him.

Daisy was in bad shape too. When Ginger Mae had refused to cooperate with Armoni, he had turned to the child, backhanding her across the face. He had knocked her into the corner of a heavy metal table and she had lain unconscious on the floor. Peter tried to make her as comfortable as possible while Armoni railed at Ginger Mae. She had come round after Peter applied a compress to her head wound, but hadn't uttered a word since. She just sat apathetically, tied to a chair next to Ginger Mae. Peter feared she might have a concussion.

He had recognized Armoni as soon as he got a good look at him. You didn't forget a face like that. He remembered the appalling moment.

"*You're* the one who came into my office, hassling my secretary, asking about Abby and Jose."

"Yeah, and I'm the one that *fucked* her too." He leered at Peter, oblivious to the saliva spraying from his mouth.

"What? What do you mean? She's dead." A sickening feeling developed in his stomach.

"Yeah, sorry about that. How'd ya think I found out where you were?" He cackled as Peter's stomach dropped to the floor. At that point, he realized they might not survive this.

It had soon became clear what Armoni wanted. He seemed to have a grudge against Abby. And the gold, of course. *I guess it always comes back to money.*

"Pay attention, college boy. I asked you if you've figured out how to get access to their bank accounts?"

"Do you mind if I take a seat?" Peter wobbled visibly, unsteady through lack of sleep, food or water. He thought he heard a click from the foyer. Attempting to draw Armoni's attention from the front of the house, he moved to a chair against the wall, away from Daisy and Ginger Mae. His heart thudded maddeningly with the slim hope that the sound might represent salvation. He prayed it might be Abby, even as he worried about drawing her into this. Maybe she had caught onto something when she visited before.

"What's it going to be, college boy? Or am I going to have to show you how serious I am?" Peter notice a golden glow coming from the foyer. He had to distract Armoni.

"You sure think you're the big man with that gun in your hand, don't you?" Peter stood as Armoni started to laugh. He reached out, punching Peter in the stomach.

"You're just lucky I need you right now, faggot, or I'd be having a party with Kelly's favorite baby all over your stupid face."

Peter coughed from the blow, trying to get his breath. In the haze of his clouded vision, a tiny funny looking creature with eyes that sparkled with swirling colors appeared, entering the kitchen from the foyer. It sported antlers that caught the light like pieces of red and black crystal. Then Abby stepped into his view. She was unarmed. *No, oh my God, what's going to happen now?*

Armoni must have sensed something. Turning, he started with welcome surprise.

"Well, well, aren't you two a sight for sore eyes. Now I won't need this dumb shit anymore." He raised the Glock and took aim at Peter.

In a split second, all hell broke loose. The creature's antlers split open, spilling out a blood-red swarm of something that hit Armoni right in the face. Before their eyes, Armoni's flesh melted down to the bone, organs and all. His skeleton teetered before crashing to the floor, still covered by the blood-red substance. When it was clear there was nothing left but bone, the substance formed into a swarm again, returning to the creature's antlers, which melded seamlessly together. A stunned silence followed.

Abby carefully walked into the room, her head turning from one to another, horror forcing her to her knees, trying to hold back dry heaves. The little creature rushed to her side as if to console her. Peter turned to Ginger Mae. She was so out of it, she probably didn't know Armoni was dead. He forced himself onto his wobbly legs, feeling like his bones had turned to liquid. With a pitiful effort, he made it over to Daisy, struggling with her restraints. She lolled passively without a sound. He picked her up, struggling with her weight, trying to contain his own adrenalin. Getting her to the sofa, he laid her down gently, collapsing at her feet as his chattering muscles gave out.

"We have to get them a doctor." He reached for Armoni's cellphone lying on the sofa table.

"No." The command came from Abby. "Put the phone down, Peter." He stared at her as if she had just said Armoni's skeleton wanted to make a call first.

"Are you out of your mind? They need a doctor. You don't know what we've been through. Did you know that man?" He could hear himself getting hysterical, the shock of what had happened finally setting in. "He was going to kill us. He was a fiend. And what the heck is that creature you have there? Where did it come from . . .? Abby, please, we need some help . . ." His voice trailed off weakly, his body slumped, burned out.

"It'll be okay, Peter. I'll see to everything." She sounded achingly tired. He watched as she got up and rummaged for a bottle and glass in his liquor cabinet. Filling it, she brought it to Peter.

"Water, please?"

She returned to Peter with the water.

"Do you think you can sew up her lip?" She gestured over to Ginger Mae. Peter looked her over, pursing his lips.

"Abby, I'm not a doctor. She needs a plastic surgeon. Why can't we call a doctor?" Abby patted his hand wearily, then dragged herself over to look at Ginger Mae. She removed her restraints and tipped her head back to see her swollen face. Peter winced at the damage caused by Armoni. Abby went to the sink, then returned with a cold cloth. As she rested it on Ginger Mae's head, she moaned. Abby wiped away the obvious blood on her face. Her lip was in bad shape but could be stitched. No one would ever refer to her as lovely again, Peter could see that. "She's coming round." Abby got up to get her some water.

"Her bruises will fade. You can stitch her lip." She fed some water to Ginger Mae and was rewarded with a demand for more. Letting her hold the glass in her unsteady hands, Abby sat down. She looked very tense, her nervous hands constantly going to her head to run her fingers through her thick white-gold hair. He saw her glance at the strange creature in the foyer. It just stood there, watching

Abby. *What the heck is it?*

"Come here, Echo." The creature made its jerky way over to Abby where it climbed up her chair, turning its head halfway around its body to give him a quick look before settling itself on Abby's lap. She put her arm around the creature and hugged it. Her lips brushed the creature's head tenderly. Together, they turned and looked at him. Abby gave him an inscrutable smile. He suddenly felt like an ant sizzling under a magnifying glass.

"Peter, this is Echo. She's an important part of our family. She just saved your butts. That fiend who was going to shoot you? That's his skeleton over there. The doctors and the cops are not going to understand when you try to tell them it beat up Ginger Mae. They'll think you did it. And they'll still want to know where the skeleton came from. I've no doubt one or all of us will wind up in jail. So I'm going to give you a choice. The cops and jail, or stitch her lip so we can get on with it. One more detail. If you choose to call the cops I can guarantee that you will die, along with the cops and everyone else in this state. Your only chance is to come with me." Taking off her glasses, Peter gawked. Abby's eyes assailed him with the same swirls of golden color as the creature's eyes. *My God, what is this?*

Peter thought his mind risked breaking. He couldn't take his eyes off her. He heard a crash and saw Ginger Mae's glass, broken on the floor, her eyes ready to pop out of her sockets. Her swollen mouth emanated meaningless sounds. Struggling to her feet she made her way to the sofa next to him and Daisy. From the foyer they heard a knock and a man's voice called out for Abby.

"In here, Cobby." Captain Cobby entered, calmly surveying the room. "When I realized something was amiss here, I called the Captain. I filled him in and he agreed to be on standby if I needed his assistance convincing you to do what was in your own best interests."

She added gently, "If you want to survive, that is. Captain Cobby will stay and answer all your questions. Echo and I need to get back to the house. Peter, I trust you ordered the extra cash for tomorrow's rescue?"

He nodded, slowly. "It's in the safe in the attic. What do we need the cash for?" Peter realized he was already calming down and coming to see the merits of her suggestion. Not hard, with a human skeleton lying in the middle of the floor.

"Bribes." Abby rose, the creature in her arms. *Echo*, he repeated the name to himself. "I will see you early in the morning, as we planned. Have Ginger Mae pack you all a bag with enough clothes for a few days. You may bring one sentimental item with you. And may I suggest a book? Take the bags down to Captain Cobby on the boat. We'll be leaving sometime after noon. Be ready or we must leave you behind. I'm going to put you in good hands. Cobby will explain further."

She rose from her seat, slipping her glasses back on. When she passed Captain Cobby, Peter watched them hug, Abby appeared to be sobbing in his arms. Straightening, she left. Captain Cobby moved into the room, making himself comfortable in the chair vacated by Abby.

"Well, my boy." Captain Cobby's voice broke with husky emotion, "How 'bout you giving us all a double shot of whatever you have in the house? It's going to be a long story and you look like you could sure use it."

Chapter 12

Abby rolled out of bed at the same time as the sun decided to yawn its rays over the eastern horizon. The stomachs of the butterflies in her stomach fluttered with their own butterflies. She got dressed and ran down the hall to wake Scotty. Echo was all ready to go, her little fanny pack strapped firmly around her waist. Abby could tell Scotty hadn't slept well, his fur was matted and ratty. His face looked as bad as a child who has discovered the fairy had forgotten to leave a dollar under his pillow after taking his tooth away.

"Come on, kiddo, up and at 'em. You look like your best friend died. We'll get through this."

After letting out the posse, Scotty fed them and lined up leashes on the terrace with boxes of dog food. He decided the posse could use Penny's doggy bed to sleep on. He didn't know how comfortable it would be for them on the boat. Returning inside for the doggie bed, he saw Chloe had left Teddy's old afghan in Penny's bed. Tossing it aside, he thought, *no time for that now.* Abby entered, carrying two bags with their clothes and a few photos of their mother. The supplies would be picked up by Kane and taken to the boat. They decided to use Scotty's Jeep for the rescue. It could hold an extra animal or two, if need be.

"Can you drive or are you too nervous?" Abby ran her hand up and down his arm for encouragement.

"I'll be okay. I can drive." Scotty met her eyes with his own. "I just don't understand how we're going to get the bears and cats to load themselves on the trucks. We need experts to handle this. What are we going to do? Say pretty please, jump on these trucks and come with us?"

"Actually, that's *exactly* what we're going to do." She smiled securely at Scotty.

"Ab, I don't think this is the time for jokes and I am sorely not in the mood." He kicked their waiting bags in anger, his eyes blazing.

Poor Scotty, she thought. *This can't be easy for him, having to leave Chloe behind.* She had done her best, trying to protect him by keeping him out of the loop. He knew nothing about what had happened at Peter's house. She could fill him in about that later, but she had better give him a few details to calm him down.

"Do you see the substance floating in Echo's antlers?" Scotty nodded. "You understand the substance had something to do with Tomas and Kelly's death?"

"Yeah, so?"

"Well, with Echo's help, I can isolate individual particles and direct them into any living creature. They enter the brain through the ear canal. They're able to interfere with the brain signals that regulate comprehension and free will. It makes them calm and easy to direct. You can control them. After Echo sends out the implants, the animal will just calmly mount the backs of the trucks and then the boat. The implants will stay in until I feel it's okay to release them. It could be years."

"Years? Why would you need to do that? Just what is really going on here, Abby? What do you mean *years*?" Scotty banged his fist on the table, making her jump. "I swear, if you don't come clean with me, *I'm not going!*"

"Okay, okay." Speaking slowly, she watched his face closely, praying he wouldn't freak out. They didn't have the time for this. "We're not going to back to Sussex, to our old home, to live there."

"For Pete's sake. Where are we going to live?"

She bowed her head, silent and overwhelmed.

"Abby," Scotty called more loudly.

Understanding, Echo interceded, her aura reaching out to envelop their minds. "Brother Scotty, the Womb has invited us all to survive the coming apocalypse in the safety of the cavern where you met me."

"*You have got to be kidding me.*"

"No, Brother Scotty, I would not do that to you. There is nothing more serious. We will have to live there for many years."

Scotty looked dumbfounded.

"Guys, we can't do that. It's ridiculous. With lions and tigers? And huge hungry bears? You've got to have a better plan than that. We can't all possibly fit in the cave where Echo hid."

"My Brother, you do not understand. I was not hiding. I lived in contemplation. And my home is not little. It is vast. The Womb will make it vaster. We have been invited. You do not understand the significance of the honor. To refuse is to perish. We must go." The aura dissipated, leaving Scotty with his mouth hanging open in alarming disbelief. Trying to suppress her fear, Abby commanded his attention. Time to move on.

"Don't forget. I need you to keep the truckers moving. Make sure they don't leave any animals behind. Echo and I will take care of implanting them as soon as we get there. We'll handle any people that we find there. I want you to lead the truckers back to the house and get the animals stashed on the boat. Don't worry if you lose us. We'll hitch a ride back with one of the truckers if we have to."

Putting a thick envelope in his hands, she said, "This is full of hundred dollar bills. Any of the truckers give you a problem, bribe them. If you run out, call me on my cell. I have more. They're all being paid very well, but you never know. When they see lions and tigers being let out of their cages, they might freak. Just make sure they get the backs of the trucks open and then get out of the way." She hugged him closely. "Are you with me?" Begrudgingly, he nodded his assent. Turning to include Echo, Abby picked her up, squeezing her tightly. "We can do this, right, Echo?"

"I have no doubt, my Sister." Echo looked up, making them both laugh, breaking the tension. She had slipped on a gift Scotty had given her. He had obtained a pair of doll's sunglasses to cover her eyes from the truckers. She now wore shades matching Abby and Scotty's. Along with her fanny pack, she looked hysterical—you had to be there.

Scotty took Echo to the garage to get the Jeep, while Abby ran next door to Peter's house. She asked him to wait in Peter's driveway while she checked on them. She wouldn't be more than five minutes. Starting the Jeep, he eased out of the garage for the last time. He could feel the late spring sun already turning into an early summer fireball, the heat turning the car into an inferno. Flipping on the air conditioner, he pulled into Peter's driveway to wait for Abby.

Abby found Peter's front door unlocked so she let herself in. She spotted three bags sitting in the foyer, just as requested. She felt some of the weight on her shoulders drain away. She wasn't sure how cooperative Peter and his girlfriend would be after the terror they'd been put through by Armoni. The shock of his death at the unnatural hand of Echo, and her subsequent revelations had only made their already fragile minds more frayed. She didn't know how reliable they were going to be today.

Entering the kitchen, she saw Ginger Mae sitting at the table, trying to get Daisy to eat, the child still nonresponsive. Ginger Mae looked up at her approach, her demeanor clearly fearful, her swollen face altering the clarity of her voice.

"Sank ou fo or help."

Abby nodded her head to indicate she understood.

"Don't try to talk. You need to save your voice and get better for Daisy. Once she's away from here and we get settled in our new home, she'll recover. I'll make sure she gets the attention she needs."

"Doctor?"

"No, not a doctor. That's not what she needs. Try not to worry." Kneeling down, Abby looked into the little girl's face, completely devoid of color, her thin hair hanging lank and limp even though Abby could smell the fresh shampoo. She spoke softly, "Hi, Daisy.

It's me. Your friend, Abby. We're going to go on a trip on my boat with some fabulous animals. We're going to go away and live with them in a magic forest near my home where I grew up. Would you like that?" Abby got no response but thought she saw a shift of the light in the child's eyes. Not much of a sign, but enough to reassure Abby that Daisy still existed in there.

Rising, she informed Ginger Mae, "I'm going to find Peter. Just nod, yes or no. Is he in his office?" Ginger Mae nodded yes. Abby rose, giving Daisy a hug, smoothing down her hair and went to find Peter.

She stood quietly at the entrance to Peter's office. He sat at his desk, his head down, buried in his arms. He must have sensed her presence because he looked up. He sat there just staring at her, saying nothing. He looked almost normal, his short-sleeved striped Oxford shirt tucked neatly into his crisp khakis. Under the desk, she could see clean leather boat shoes. Looking into his expressionless face, she could see his eyes were doing some strange jerky motions, his blinking frantic. *Well,* she thought, *he's certainly not back to normal.*

"Are you going to be okay, Peter?"

"Why don't you sit down, Abby?"

"I don't have time. Scotty's waiting for me in the car. And Echo."

"Echo," he repeated.

"Yes, we'll be gone for about four hours, then return with the animals. Please try to be in your cabin onboard by then. Take one of the aft cabins for the three of you. We won't be on the boat for long. Just until we get to Tampa and transfer to the airport. But I think Ginger Mae and Daisy might need to rest. It'll keep them from getting underfoot. Once we arrive, things will be chaotic until we cast off. Was Cobby able to answer most of your questions?" She tried to sound reassuring.

"For now." He sounded far from reassured. Impulsively, she went to his side. She pulled up a chair from alongside the hand-painted wall. Sitting, she rested her hands on the desk next to his.

"Please, Peter. Please try to understand. I'm just a young girl who lost her mother barely a year ago. I didn't even have a chance to mourn her before I had this nightmare thrust on me. I didn't ask for it. I'm still not over the horror of my body changing, or the realization that something so terrible is going to happen that millions will die. Hundreds of millions. I can't handle this kind of responsibility, but I have to think of my family. And Jose doesn't even know about it yet. So I keep putting one foot in front of the other to ensure our safety. I regret your involvement but I needed your help. In time, you'll learn to be grateful. Ginger and Daisy are your family now."

"She's *not* my family."

Wow, she thought, *finally a reaction*. Something must have happened. She wondered if it had anything to do with Armoni.

"She's a woman you care about with a child who needs your support. One foot in front of the other, Peter. I have to go now. I know you'll do the right thing." Giving him a kiss on his sweating cheek, she ran out to meet Scotty.

The Jeep felt nice and cool as she slid inside. A quick glance at her watch spurred her on; already the time relentlessly ran ahead of her. She chose the parking lot at the mall on Tamiami Trail as the staging area for the trucks. Large trucks would blend in at the mall, appearing to belong there to deliver merchandise, drawing no unwanted attention. Leaving Peter's driveway, they hurried off the key to the highway to find the traffic fairly light, rush hour not yet upon them.

As they pulled into the mall parking lot, it was easy to spot the trucks, their drivers loosely gathered around in a huddle as they anxiously watched cars entering the parking lot, probably looking for their benefactor. *That's good*, Abby thought. She hoped some of them had tried to hold onto the jobs they had previously lined up before Peter called them. They knew this gig was a quickie. If they were in a hurry, they would be less likely to ask questions. They would be tempted to keep their heads down, get the job done and skate out fast to salvage their original job.

Abby jumped out of the Jeep to introduce herself. She looked into the faces of the road-worn men and women, the backbone of what kept this country's faltering commerce functioning. She found it incomprehensible to believe they would all be dead in the very near future, the truth forcing her to evade their eyes, grateful for her sunglasses. One of the truckers held up his hand with a question. An older man with a heavy gut flopping over his pants so much she wondered how his jeans stayed up. *Here it comes,* Abby thought. If she couldn't handle the questions, she would be forced to use Echo to implant them, but Echo had told her the implants interfered with the part of the brain that controlled hand-to-eye coordination; a huge drawback if you needed to drive. *What's the point of trying to rescue the animals only to endanger them with a possible driving accident?*

"Miss Preston? Clyde Calloway here. I understand we're here to move some animals? You mind telling us what kind of animals?"

"Well, Mr. Calloway, they're wild animals. You won't need to participate in the loading. Just open the trucks and step out of the way. Loading will take a little more than an hour. Then we'll drive to the coast, about half an hour away. Unloading will be simple. Again, just open the trucks and step out of the way. My attorney will be on site later to see that your bonuses are all paid."

She got a smattering of applause and hoots on the word bonus. The truckers scrambled to their rigs and fired up the ones that were not already idling. In a matter of minutes, the caravan of a dozen trucks hit the road, heading to the Big Cat Sanctuary, the Jeep in the lead.

As Scotty led the caravan toward the sanctuary, Abby speculated on what it took to create such a beautiful facility for the Earth's abused, exploited and discarded wildlife. What kind of self-sacrifice did it take to put an animal's needs before your own or that of your family's? Did it take a spiritual person to demand the dedication? Was it a thankless journey? She didn't think so. It was probably reward enough to wake up every day to look into the content innocent eyes of some of God's most awe-inspiring creatures. They were all victims. Innocent victims of man's hubris and unlimited capacity to exploit any and all of the planet's resources to the point of destruction. But not all men. She was always amazed when she read stories of someone risking their own life in the rescue of an animal. Like Scotty and Echo. It gave her hope. She had always thought there might be a chance for man to redeem himself. Unfortunately, and unexpectedly, man was now out of time. She wiped away a lonely tear, shaking off her melancholy thoughts. It no longer mattered with the impending tragedy looming.

Abby wondered what descendants remained of the original circus family who had started the sanctuary. Would they approve of what she planned to do with their precious charges? *I think they would.* Was it any different than the terrified mother, caught in a raging apartment fire who begs the fireman to save her infant as the fire consumes her home? Well, I'm just the fireman come to rescue their babies before the fire rages at the feet of humanity.

Abby glanced at Scotty, seeing his tight lips and white knuckles on the steering wheel. She reached over to give him a squeeze, and was rewarded with a tentative smile.

"Why us, Abby? Why did it have to be us? Was it because I found the old gold coin when I was a boy?"

"If it hadn't have been us, I would still be sick. I might not ever have fallen in love with Jose." Smiling at him, she spoke softly. "You never would have met Chloe." Sobering, she reminded him, "And worst of all, we would have all been killed anyway. I still don't know what's going to happen, but I feel a more desperate sense of urgency. We must get back home to Sussex as quickly as possible. Jose and Mama Diaz will be waiting for us."

"Is there anything else we can do to convince Chloe to come with us? I asked her, but I couldn't very well tell her the whole story. Abby, could you give her a call?" He was begging.

"I don't know what I can say that you left out. You know we can't tell her the truth. We could give her an implant, but that would be like kidnapping her. She has to come willingly, hon."

Scotty greeted her words with silence. Abby gave him a quick look. He appeared pensive, not crestfallen or even sulking as she would have expected. Noticing her watching him, he turned his attention to the road. Letting the subject drop, she also faced the road as they made their way to their destination.

It wasn't long before they pulled up in front of the gate blocking their passage onto the gravel road which would take them up to the enclosures. Reaching into the back of the SUV, Scotty grabbed a pair of bolt cutters he had stashed on the back seat a few days ago at Abby's request. He hurried up to the gate, snapping the chain before any of the drivers were the wiser. He quickly opened the gates, wedging them open with bricks he found, conveniently left by some absentminded grounds tender.

They were in. The convoy rolled onto the property. Abby cringed at the noise the trucks made on the gravel driveway, dust swirling up and over the animal enclosures in opaque clouds. Scotty parked the Jeep and directed the trucks to line up back down the dusty drive, facing the gate for a quick and easy getaway. The drivers began to open the back of their trucks. The plan called for Scotty to position himself at the first enclosure. Abby and Echo, from the relative privacy of the Jeep, would send out Echo's implants–they were trying to shelter Echo's presence from the truckers. Scotty would then open the enclosures with his bolt cutters, snapping the padlocks. Each animal would be directed by its implant to find a truck and enter, while Abby would spend the time keeping the truckers under control. Echo would stay out of sight in the Jeep unless someone from the sanctuary showed up. Then she would send implants out to subdue them. Abby watched as she saw Echo's antlers split open, sending the implants on their way to find their wildlife targets.

"Miss Preston, we're ready for the cargo." The driver of the truck closest to the Jeep came around the back of the truck to make his announcement. A skinny young fellow with a face like a weasel, a tiny sprout of hair on his chin, trying hard to look like one of the boys. He sported a cigarette between his fingers as he leaned casually against the truck sucking on his cancer stick. Abby noticed Scotty moving on to the second bear enclosure. Lumbering out of the first enclosure appeared a six-hundred-pound brown bear. *Oh, boy . . .*

"Sir, I have to ask you to remain in your cab until we are completely loaded." Abby's voice spiked sharply with anxiety. The trucker lazily tossed his butt to the ground, twisting his foot over it.

"Okay, okay, no need to get your panties in a—*what the fuck?*" The trucker backed up against the truck as if bitten, freezing as the brown bear calmly walked past him to trudge up the metal incline into the back of the truck, where he pawed at the pile of blankets Abby had ordered for their comfort, making a nice nest for himself, then curling up to placidly watch the rest of the action. Right behind the brown bear lumbered two more large bears. The thunderstruck trucker forgot to move.

Next, a male lion padded his way, his thick, dark mane making him look like the true king of the savanna. Speechless, the trucker's face caved in, looking as pinched as if he had just finished sucking on a hard green lemon. Carefully he backed up to the door of his cab, clambering up as if goosed by the devil himself.

Abby turned away from the now secured trucker to monitor the animals as Scotty released them from their cages. Scanning the line of trucks, she could see the animals sort themselves into them with no rhyme or reason.

She peeked into one truck down the line that contained a bear and a tiger sitting placidly with a group of goats and two spider monkeys. She found herself sweating about the combination, hoping nothing would go wrong with the implant control. She held her breath as she felt a Siberian tiger brush past her to the next truck. She noticed he had a piece missing from his left ear, near the tip. Her heart was in her throat as the magnificent beast turned his head and met her gaze. She backed away as he turned, continuing on to the next truck. She put her hand to her tripping heart in an instinctive effort to slow it down. Breathing slowly and deeply, her heart stopped its painful ratcheting. She shook her head, trying to shake off the hypnotic feeling she had received from the tiger. *Wow. What was that all about?*

Hurrying down the line of trucks, she banged on the cab doors of each truck containing a complete load, instructing the drivers to close up and get ready to roll. Running back to the SUV, she saw the door pop open on the house she assumed would contain sanctuary personnel. Tapping on the side of the Jeep, she noticed Echo's head pop up.

"Hit anyone that comes out of that house, okay, girl?"

Echo nodded her head as her antlers peeled back, releasing a tiny stream of implants. Two women and a man rushed out of the house shouting, their features suffused in anger. The man carried a rifle at his side. As the implants landed, making their way into their ears, they came to a halt. Abby walked over to them, watching carefully as they adjusted to the implants. The women both stood tall and lean, their hair pulled back in thick black ponytails, similar enough to be a mother-daughter team. The short bald man lacked any resemblance to the women, and his Asian eyes were ready to pop out of his skull.

"My name is Abby. I would like to have that rifle, please." The man smiled and handed the rifle to her without a peep. "Please go over to the tortoise enclosure and make sure they find a comfortable spot on a truck. If you can't find any room, let me know. Do you understand?"

"Of course, Abby, we're happy to help." Smiles plastered dumbly on their blank faces, they trotted off to get the giant tortoises. Ruefully shaking her head, she laughed with irony at how happy they were to help. She wished she had thought of that earlier. It certainly took the sting out of the appearance that they were stealing the animals. Stashing the rifle in the Jeep under the seat, she ran through the compound, shouting for Scotty. She spotted him in the field with the camels. As he caught up to her, the trailing camels lingered alongside. Scotty gave the leader an extra swat on the rump to hurry them along to the trucks.

"How're we doing?" Scotty asked.

"Things are going well. Much easier than I thought. Echo implanted three people from the sanctuary who showed up unexpectedly. They're actually helping to load the trucks. They're working on the tortoises right now."

"Cool. I guess we're almost done. But Abby, don't we need food for these guys? I don't want any of those cats to get hungry."

"Don't worry. Got that covered. The implants will suppress the enzymes that regulate the hunger signals, just as their natural reaction to prey is being suppressed. They won't suffer unless they don't get food within a few days. We'll have plenty of water available. I guess we're in good shape."

"Uh oh—we've got a problem." Scotty peered over Abby's shoulder toward a small ramshackle house trailer on the edge of the compound. Abby assumed the food preparation station was in the trailer and hadn't checked it out.

"Let me handle this. You go check on the truckers," Abby said. "Make sure we're almost ready to roll. I'll swing through the enclosures as soon as I'm finished here." Nodding, and with one last glance at the house trailer, Scotty ran off.

Abby kept her eyes on the steps of the trailer as she made her way toward the young girl standing there. She looked to be about seventeen or eighteen, a well-endowed light-skinned black girl with stunningly long shapely legs being shown to their best advantage in her tiny white linen shorts. Her rich dark curly hair, spiking out in an unbelievable corona around her face and down her back, dwarfed her slender frame. Her dark almond eyes settled on Abby as she approached, a slight smile on the perfect curves of her luscious lips.

"What's up, chicky? Where you takin' all the kitties?"

Hmm, sassy, Abby thought, watching her big gold hoops flash in her ears to the rhythm of her words. Abby stood at the bottom of the steps looking up.

"You work here? What's your name?" Abby could now see her huge abdomen. She looked to be about five months, maybe more. Hard to tell with such a slender figure.

"My name's Kenya. Kenya McCready. And who you be, chicky?" She stood with one hand on her hip, looking annoyed. "I just finished chopping a ton of greens and fruit for all a them turtles, and they can eat. You takin' them too?"

"Yes, we are."

"Well, what the heck am I gonna do with all a these greens?" She took out her cell and dialed a number. Abby stood, not knowing what to do with this unexpected young lady. She looked around for Scotty, hoping he was on his way with Echo. She glanced at Kenya's expanding midriff, wondering what impact an implant might have on a fetus. Kenya spoke into her cell.

"Sandra, can ya call me back and let me know what I'm supposed ta do with the greens I been slavin' over? The lady's here for the turtles." Closing her cell, she said, "Don't that beat all. I don't know why somebody didn't let me know. Well, I'll tell you, chicky, I'm makin' damn sure I get full credit for my hours. I only have ten left and I'm done. No more community service. Done, finished, kaput. Won't be seein' my black booty round here no more." Focusing her attention back on Abby, she said, "So who's that cute hottie I just saw you with, chicky?" She threw one hip up on the short porch railing, swinging her leg casually, as if she had all the time in the world to gossip.

"That's my brother, Scott. I'm Abby." She made a quick decision. She couldn't leave Kenya here with the others who were under the influence of the implants. Once they left she would realize something didn't jibe. All she had to do was talk to them. Kenya looked pretty street smart. They couldn't risk her calling the cops.

"You're supposed to come with us. Sorry, I didn't know you were Kenya, the girl I was told to look for."

Hopping down from her perch, Kenya squinted at Abby. "Where we supposed ta go?"

"Bird Key. It's about twenty minutes from here near the bridge."

Kenya's haughty face relaxed. "I ain't no dummy. I know where that is. Very muckity-muck." Kenya pranced down the steps to face Abby.

"Well, it's almost time to leave. You can come with us in the Jeep. My brother will be driving." Abby walked to the Jeep, hoping Kenya wouldn't ask any more questions. Scotty started when he spotted Kenya as he returned from checking the trucks.

"We're all set, Ab." He raised his eyebrows, nodding toward Kenya.

"Scotty, this is Kenya, she's going to ride with us. She's supposed to give us a hand with the animals." She turned to Kenya, who stood smiling at Scotty, preening and tossing her magnificent mane.

"Scotty will take you anywhere you need to go when we're done. Okay?"

"Yeah, sure, chicky, whatever you say." She placed her hand on the door. Swinging it open, she slid her ample abdomen up on the seat, right next to Echo, seemingly not even noticing her.

Abby and Scotty hurried to the front seats as the trucks revved their idling engines. The three sanctuary workers walked right past the Jeep toward the house. Kenya stuck her head out the window, hollering, and waved.

"Sandra, I'll see ya next week. Don't forget ta mark my hours, now." The three of them waved back and returned to the house. Abby visibly relaxed. Scotty pulled out alongside the trucks and proceeded down the gravel drive to take the lead. Pulling beyond the sanctuary gates, they headed for Bird Key.

"Uh . . . hey, chickies." Kenya stuck her head up between Scotty and Abby, whispering loudly and talking as if they didn't understand English. "Did-you-know-there's-a-creature-in-the-back-seat-with-me? Ain't no creature I ever seen before. Does it bite?" She looked worried.

"No, she doesn't have any teeth," Abby answered. Kenya gave Echo another good look. Sticking her head up between the seats again, she whispered, "Did you know it's wearing a pair of sunglasses? And a tiny old-fashioned fanny pack? What's up with that? I don't ever see no creatures dressed like that, 'cept the chimp, that is. They dress him up like a baby all the time."

Scotty spoke up. "She has a name—Echo. She's just a family pet that we have fun dressing up. I'm into fashion." Abby rolled her eyes at Scotty.

"Fashion? I think we have a lot in common, Scott. We'll have to compare notes." She pinched his arm, winked and then glanced at Abby. "When I finish working and all, that is." Abby began to wonder just who this irreverent young girl was.

"Where do you live, Kenya?"

"I'm from Sarasota, believe or not. I'm from the project. Over by Martin Luther King Boulevard. The only one in the whole town." She lowered her voice with a trace of bitterness. "I live in a group home for the unwed. Can't be on my own till I turn eighteen. Won't be long now. Then me and my baby will find us a nice fly guy with a big ole house that gots a yard for my baby and a first-rate set a wheels." She was beaming over her big plans.

"Where's your mom and dad?" Abby assumed they would want to be there when the baby came. "And the baby's daddy, I take it he's no longer in the picture?"

Kenya laughed. "He was never even *in* the picture. Don't know my daddy, my momma got shot when I was five. Not too many nice ladies want to adopt a five-year-old. They want an infant. The ladies round hereabouts wants a white baby. But don' you worry 'bout me. I'm gonna have my own family, jus' soon as my baby born." She rubbed her belly, a dreamy expression on her elegant face. Abby wondered exactly how hard this poor kid had been raised. And by who?

"So, Kenya, why are you doing community service?"

Kenya sighed, her arms wrapping tighter around her belly. "I hit a girl. She stole my baby clothes I been savin' for. She went right into my dresser and took em. Probably sold em for a couple a bucks for her skag. I don't make much money at the sanctuary. Been workin' there for one ta two years. Sandra worked it out with the judge after that thievin' bitch signed a complaint against me, that I could do my service at the sanctuary. I don't start getting paid again till my service is done. Sandra's a nice lady. She knows I love animals. They don't judge me or leave me. Sandra's tryin' ta work out me livin' at the big house after the baby comes. Sure is good of her, but she don't understand. I need to find me a fly guy for my baby. I'm not letting my baby grow up like a vagabond. We deserve to make a family."

You sure do, Abby thought. "I know just what you mean, Kenya. You keep your chin up and do what you have to do for the baby."

Scotty gave her a thumb's up sign and she winked at him again.

Chapter 13

Lita zipped up her fly. Tucking her blue and white cotton checkered shirt into her jeans, she surveyed her bedroom to see if she had overlooked anything. She was the happiest she'd been since Omar Nasir had called to announce his demands for her attention. She found it very difficult to beg off without making him suspicious. *Damn. Just when I'd finally found myself on the cusp of a new life.* She had been all set to ship her furniture north and disappear when she had made the mistake of answering her cell without checking to identify the caller first. *Trapped.*

The days with him at the Ritz Carlton had crawled unbearably. She had even less tolerance for him now, knowing she was only a hairbreadth away from getting a real life back. She felt the pain he inflicted on her more intensely. She found it harder to smile and beguile him. She loathed his selfish, egotistical, demeaning, chauvinistic, condescending, misogynistic . . . *did I leave out the fact that he possesses a small dick—thank heavens–and frequently reeks of body odor?*

She laughed deliciously for the first time in almost a decade. Yes, she thought, that's how freedom tastes. She made a note to call her parents. They would be ecstatic. She lived with many restrictions when undercover and her communications with her parents suffered. They didn't even know where she lived. Slipping into her sneakers, she heard the doorbell ring. Frowning, she realized the movers were here, albeit early. Didn't matter. She was raring to go.

Grabbing her purse, she took out the engagement ring Omar had given her. She didn't doubt the significant value of the diamond. Slipping it back into her purse, she decided she would sell it and give the proceeds to the scholarship fund offered by the company for children of agents killed in the field. The doorbell rang again. The movers. She ran to answer it, dancing on air.

Omar Nasir prepared for his long-awaited meeting with the imams. It was still early in the morning, the Florida sun just starting its relentless pounding on the hapless inhabitants who had failed to escape to their essential air conditioning. He stretched out on his deceased wife's comfortable antique fainting sofa in their bedroom. He found it difficult to get motivated, still mystified as to the imams' agenda.

He tried, discreetly, to put feelers out within his network as to the purpose of the meeting. He didn't doubt that the news of his engagement had reached them by now. That should make them very happy, as they pressured him incessantly to take a wife to the White House. They wanted him to appeal to the parts of the country which revered family and traditional values, which was not the normal Socialist New World Party's base.

The imams wanted to make sure that everyone loved and trusted him, so the public wouldn't see the end coming. Twenty years in the planning, one must admire their patience. And the respect they commanded. Their tentacles reached far and wide. Very wide. Unfortunately, he too must always be on his toes, never knowing who watched, or from where.

Thinking of his engagement, he turned his mind to Lita. She had genuinely seemed shocked when he had presented her with the ring, sliding it on her finger to proclaim his possession. He did not actually *propose*. A ridiculous American tradition, asking for the woman's permission. Humiliating. Besides, a Syrian woman would not expect it. She knew her duty and the behavior required of her in their relationship.

He must admit that their time at the Ritz Carlton had fallen a little flat. Her lovemaking had lacked her usual level of passion. *And what had happened to the exciting conversationalist I always enjoyed?*

When he inquired, she indifferently chalked it up to her allergies.

Feeling hungry for his breakfast, he called down to the kitchen to inquire about the delay. Oddly, no one picked up his call, a very rare occurrence. He decided to try again in a few minutes.

Rising to use the bathroom, he caught a glimpse of himself in the vanity mirror. Was that more gray? Moving up close to the mirror, he ran his hairy fingers over his well-developed chest, liking the look and feel of his thick thatch of dark hair. But he didn't like the strands of gray that had suddenly appeared on his well-coiffed head. It must be all the stress. Now in his late forties, he found he worried more. And he always seemed to be tired. Maybe from the constant campaigning? He couldn't wait for November when it would all be over.

He wondered what date he should set for the wedding. Maybe after the election. A White House wedding sounded elegant. They could get it out of the way before the next phase of the imams' plan was initiated: using him to smuggle in the bombs, the details still unknown to him. Well, they would tell him soon enough.

He glanced at his watch. Where was his breakfast? He wanted to eat before he put on his disguise. He called the kitchen again. Still no answer. *Where was that woman?* His cook had been with him for over ten years, provided by Andrew. Andrew Brooks did all the hiring of the guards and house staff.

Andrew's talents made his world manageable: Brooks was his most invaluable confidant and his closest associate. Odd, considering he knew very little about Andrew's own life. Yet Andrew knew everything about him. Oh well, *his* importance overruled all other considerations, especially trivial affairs of his employees and associates.

Tired of ruminating, he decided to don his disguise and head down to the boat. He would check the kitchen on the way out, but he no longer had time to eat. He would have to wait for lunch.

He took his time applying his makeup and hairpieces, fingers expertly fashioning his new persona. Nasir made a mental note to have Andrew obtain a cane for him. Hunching over with no support just to further his disguise hurt his back. The cane would give him support and add to his elderly persona.

Peering out his bedroom window, he observed the morning heat shimmering off the flagstone terrace, his daughter already swimming in the pool. He should be back in time to have lunch with her. That would be a nice treat.

He reached for his cell again. He wanted to call Lita before he set off in the boat. Waiting impatiently for her to pick up, he smiled at the thought of how handsome he would look on their wedding day, with her at his side. She did not pick up her cell. Now, he was starting to steam. *Why are people not responding?*

Donning his geriatric clothes, he started briskly down the back staircase, directly to the kitchen. Further annoyed, he found the kitchen empty. The long gleaming stainless steel and granite countertops were spotless. No pots simmered on either the red Wolf range, or the chocolate Viking; its six burners were cold, the grill empty. Leaving a note for the cook regarding his lunch with his daughter, he hurried out the back door, skirting the pool and going directly to the waiting boat.

Boarding the Bertram, he ordered his waiting man to cast off.

"Where are the rest of the men? They knew I needed to go to the mainland."

The pilot shrugged his shoulders. "I don't know, sir, but I am at your disposal."

Omar grumbled and steamed. So far the day had been determined to conspire against him.

Making himself comfortable in a flowered outdoor chair, he watched his man pilot the boat across the bay, sunlight reflecting off the cold ocean water, blinding his sight. He raised his hand to shelter his eyes, his false bifocals prohibiting the use of sunglasses.

His man turned and gave him a quick look. Their eyes accidently met. *What the f— was that look on his face?* Squinting, Omar could swear the man's eyes flashed contempt at him. *How dare he?* If he could afford the time he would discipline the man himself. He must speak to Andrew Brooks about him when he returned to the estate, then dismissed him immediately from his thoughts.

Before long they docked at Marina Jack's. Nasir quickly disembarked, getting a nod from his man.

"Do not leave the boat. I will be back within the hour."

"Yes sir."

Omar turned away slowly, giving the man a long look. He could swear he could still see something different in the man's eyes. *The man will soon rue the day he crossed my path.* Hurrying across the street, he walked quickly to the mosque.

He entered, removing his sandals in the antechamber before being quickly ushered past the prayer room down a long hall to the rear of the mosque. Swarthy bearded men milled around the door behind which the imams waited. He entered, respect radiating from his every subservient gesture.

The small stark room housed a low metal table at which the three gaunt imams sat in their robes, their long gray beards resting in their laps. Their eyes projected a fierce calm. Behind the imams, an oak sideboard held a slight pile of papers. Two aides waited reverently in the corner of the room near the only window, open to the courtyard. After exchanging traditional greetings, the aides signaled Omar to sit on the cushion across from the middle imam.

He hurriedly made himself comfortable, waiting for them to begin. No one spoke. Omar looked from one to the other as they appeared to study him. A prickly sensation distracted him, making the hairs on his back itch. He felt his hands turn to ice . . . *something's wrong.* Imam Mohammed al Qua Terique turned and reached for the papers on the sideboard, holding them against his chest. A sudden premonition knifed cleanly through Omar's bowels.

"You have been a fool, Omar."

More silence, his heart hammered, draining his face of all color. "I don't understand, your—"

"Shut up, you fool. You have ruined twenty years of interminable planning. Many men have risked much to make this happen. The Salafis have waited so long, and are finally in position to eliminate the western devil. All ruined over a woman." He spat on the table, throwing down a ring and a photo. "Pick them up and look at your whore."

Omar's hands shaking, he picked up the photo and the engagement ring he had put on Lita's finger just days ago. He focused on the photo. She lay on the floor of what appeared to be her bedroom, panties wrapped around her neck, her body nude. Signs of rape. Her hands were tied and bound to a leg of the bed he had used so many times to enjoy her tasty body. Above her once beautiful eyes sat the ugly bullet hole that had ended her life.

He closed his eyes, stalling for time. *Why did they do this?* His mind spiraled with questions. His bowels groaned uneasily. "Why was this necessary? You approved the relationship."

The imam flicked his finger on the remaining photo, sliding it toward Omar. He picked it up. It showed Lita in a pantsuit, her luscious hair drawn back in a youthful ponytail with none of the exotic cosmetics she normally wore. She stood on a street in front of an Asian grocery, looking like any other American woman. He peered closer . . . American? He looked up questioningly.

"She is CIA, you fool. This was taken in New York City over two weeks ago. The grocery is a front for the CIA head field office. Did you even know she was in New York?"

Omar's shock was palpable as he shook his head slowly. "She was fully vetted. She's clean. She's from Syria," he whispered.

"She is *American,*" the imam roared, slapping his hands on the table, making Omar jump. Silence descended in the small room. Omar could feel a bead of sweat roll down the side of his temple. He wondered if he would get out of the mosque alive. His only hope might be the fact that they wouldn't dare draw attention to the mosque which served as a cover for their activities. If they tried to take him outside, he might have a chance to escape. He pushed the thoughts of his tired body and pampered lifestyle away from his hope of escape.

"They must have known of our plans for years." The bitterness cut deep in the fanatic's voice. "Our only hope is to revamp and move our operation to *go* status. In the last two weeks we have made alternative plans. Two neutron bombs are making their way over the border from Mexico. They should have arrived on the U.S. side by now. They will be airborne in a dozen hours." The three imams rose. "We are leaving for the airport now. We will be in Cairo by this evening." Omar's mind swam with confusion.

"What do you want me to do?" He cringed at the whining tone of his voice, visions of his presidential inauguration dissolving. Mohammed al Qua Terique eyed him disdainfully, his contempt crystal clear.

"I suggest you start running." He turned and left the room, the other imams and the aides scurrying behind. Omar waited a few minutes to let the imams clear out of the mosque. He tried to slow the frantic thundering of his heart so he could think. He must get home to collect his daughter. The safe in his study contained enough cash to save them both.

He carefully peered out into the hallway, finding it empty. He ran down the deserted hall to the prayer room where he slowed down. Entering the antechamber, he searched for his sandals. No one stopped him. Not bothering with the stooped posture of his disguise, he hurried back to Marina Jack's. He ran down the dock to the Bertram, but his man was nowhere to be seen. *Damn. The idiot was probably sucking up a beer at the bar.* Racing over to the marine bar he looked around wildly for his pilot, losing precious time.

Abandoning the Bertram, he made a quick call to the house. No one picked up. He called Brooks. Nothing. He paced madly, his cell to his ear. Frustration began to overwhelm him. He stopped pacing and drew a deep breath. Again. More able to think, he decided to call for a cab. His luck held. A cab pulled up to valet parking in front of Marina Jack's formal restaurant, the patrons entering, well-heeled and dressed to kill, their beautiful well-maintained faces laughing and joyful, were oblivious to the coming destruction.

He slid into the back of the cab, spitting out his address. His heart began to hammer again, sweat dripping from both temples. He loosened his collar trying for air. The driver watched him from the rearview mirror.

"You okay, buddy?"

"Yeah," he gulped. "Just drive, I'm in a hurry." Thinking of Lita's beautiful face marred by the ugly hole in her head left him full of rage. If she was here, he would shoot her himself. *The fucking American cunt.* His blood boiled with the thought of how she must have laughed at him behind his back with her co-conspirators.

He suddenly realized he had no money in his pockets. No worries, he could get the cab fare from his man at the gate. He wondered who manned the gate today. Should he tell the help? Rejecting the idea, he knew he didn't have the time to explain.

Quickly dialing his bank, he requested a wire transfer to the National Trust of Switzerland in Zurich. He watched the driver's eyes pop in the rearview window when he mentioned the amount. As they pulled up to his house, he felt a buzz in his head. The gates were wide open and no one sat in the guardhouse. They driver pulled up to the front door. Jumping out, he ordered the driver to wait. He could take them to the airport.

Running up to his daughter's room, he barged in. She looked up from the floor where she was brushing her dog. *Oh God, the dog's going to be a problem. She'll want to take him.*

"Hi, baby." He rushed to her closet, taking down a piece of luggage. "You have to pack. It's an emergency. Pack light. We can replace anything you need later. Your pup has to stay behind. We can't take him. He'll slow us down." He saw she was still on the floor, holding the pup he had given her closely.

"Where are we going, Daddy?"

"To Switzerland for now." He started to pull open her dresser drawers. "Come on, baby. We have to go. Put the dog down."

"Daddy, I can't leave him. He has to come." She was going to give him a problem about that damn dog. *I ought to wring its neck right now.*

"Okay, we'll deal with him later. I need you to pack now. I'll be down the hall packing if you need me."

"How long will we be gone?"

"We're not coming back." Too late, he realized he probably shouldn't have said that.

"I don't understand. My swim trials are coming up in a few weeks. Is Uncle Andrew coming too?"

"Honey, I don't know. Let me go so I can make some arrangements. Have you seen your Uncle Andrew today?" He was at the door, ready to bolt down the hall.

"No, Daddy."

"Come on, baby. Get up and pack. *Now.*" Turning, he dashed out the door to find Andrew.

It didn't take him long to realize they were alone in the house, the help nowhere to be found. He didn't need this additional complication, now of all times. He descended the main staircase to the foyer. Walking to the back of the house, he passed the monkey cages and turned, entering his study. He went right to the library shelves. Pushing aside a line of popular junk bestsellers—*who would bother checking behind them?*—he exposed his safe.

Spinning the dial, he opened the door, pulled out his papers and the stacks of cash, shoving them into a plastic bag that he would pack into his briefcase upstairs. His eyes, engrossed in the papers, failed to notice an obstacle on the floor. Moving to his desk, he tripped over something bulky, sending him falling to the floor, landing on his elbow, his papers and money spreading all over a dead body. Springing back from the cold body, his mind refused to register the horror before him.

He froze, hearing the click of a handgun. Looking up from the floor, he looked into the grim face of Andrew Brooks, his trusted long-time, right-hand man who stood pointing a gun at him, his eyes filled with ironic amusement.

Chapter 14

Jose's plane landed at Sarasota Airport late in the morning. He was anxious to surprise Abby, but worried about her insistence that he go home to Sussex and wait for her there. He fully intended to get to the bottom of her bizarre behavior. Only then could he have Mama Diaz and the girls move down to Florida with them. This overriding goal pressured him to quickly reunite what was left of his adopted family. This insistence they go to Sussex was nothing short of bizarre, yet Abby had refused to discuss the issue on her cell.

Grabbing a cab after he got off the plane, he gave the cabbie his address. Sitting back, he realized his anger about the whole thing with Abby still hovered under the surface. He thought back two weeks ago when he had left for New Jersey, hoping he would be returning victoriously to Florida.

It hadn't taken very long to find them. The excellent investigators had finally produced results. Scotty had driven to the Short Hills tenement as soon as he had obtained the address. Mama Diaz burst out crying as soon as she opened the door to find him there. He took her in his arms trying to kiss her tears away, observing how her formerly thick chestnut hair felt thin and was shot heavily with gray, her laugh lines now etched deep and permanent. Pulling him into the apartment, she insisted on making him tea while they caught up on family news.

While Mama Diaz made the tea, he looked around the tiny one-bedroom apartment. The girls shared the bedroom and Mama Diaz slept on the sad, ugly sofa in their combination living room/kitchen. As he stood on the chipped linoleum floor, he took note of the bars on the one window in the apartment. The kitchen boasted a substandard-sized refrigerator, a white stove and a scratched white enamel sink built into appalling chipboard cabinets and linoleum countertop. Set on the wall over the kitchen table, Mama Diaz's own crucifix from Lily Pond Road proudly graced the wall. He hoped her religion provided her with great comfort because she sure wasn't getting it from the dump they lived in. His blood boiled when he thought about the house waiting for her and the girls in Florida.

Mama Diaz set the tea down on the table. Jose pulled out a rickety chair for her, urging her to sit.

"Mama, I need to know. Why did you move to Short Hills? I don't understand."

"Jose, you're such a good boy. I couldn't have Bonnie and Emma live in the pigsty my Tomas took us to. He knew better. Something was definitely not right with my Tomas. I think he just wanted us out of the way." She shook her head, pain etched in her weary eyes.

"And there's this Armoni. Did you know about Kelly's brother? The man is hideous. I couldn't have him around the girls. It boggles the mind that my boy took us there. I did think about coming back home but Tomas said we had to leave you alone. He said Abby was glad to get her house back. I couldn't barge in on you kids. The very next day he brought us here. It's better than being at Kelly's house. Tomas paid for the first month's rent and the security. He took us to the grocery store, and then we never saw him again. He just left us here.

"I found a job at a grocery store fifteen blocks from here. I got the girls into a school with some decent teachers. They seem to be as happy as can be expected under the circumstances. Emma has a part-time job in the nursing home a few blocks away. She works on weekends. I applied for public assistance last week. I should hear soon. It will be such a big help."

The tears slipped silently from Jose's eyes. He put his arms around his adopted mother. They cried together.

"It's over, I'm here now. We found you. You'll come to live with us." Jose held her as he told her of their new life. He told her about everything except their isolation and the secrecy.

After having tea, Mama Diaz and Jose went to the grocery store to buy treats for a surprise celebratory dinner. They bought fresh meat and vegetables, as well as bacon—an unheard-of treat—not to mention cupcakes and ice cream. Their giddiness and excitement about the future allowed Mama Diaz to laugh and exclaim over the sinful extravagances. Jose had so much fun showering Mama Diaz with goodies that everyone in the store watched them enviously. Such a sign of prosperity was very unusual in their neighborhood.

Loading their purchases in Jose's rental car, they talked about the upcoming science project at Emma's school.

"She is very proud of her work, an elaborate diorama of the creatures which the planet has lost through extinction in the last one hundred years. Emma is very artistic. She did all the drawing and models herself. Her project won't be presented for another week. I think it would mean a lot to her if we could wait until she presented her project before we leave. Do you think we can wait that long?" Mama Diaz looked anxious as she unpacked the luxuries from the market.

"Mama, we can wait as long as you guys need. We've waited this long. What's another week?"

When the girls came home from school, he winced at how ragged they looked. It took him awhile to realize it was exactly how they had all looked when they lived together on Lily Pond Road. They lived so differently in Sarasota that the contrast was painful.

Emma had finally found a growth spurt, and was now a spirited yet serious young lady. Bonnie, still very young, her short curly brown hair framing her round impish face had yet to lose her baby fat even though she stood to finish her freshman year of high school soon. As much as he missed Abby, with Mama and the girls he felt surrounded by a feeling of home. And it wasn't because he was back in New Jersey. It was because this was a vital and missing part of his life. He didn't get this feeling in Sarasota. He needed it. They all needed it. It just made him more anxious to get everyone safely back to Florida.

Not surprisingly, the description of Jose, Abby and Scotty's new life shocked them all. The girls went wild, excited over the possibilities. Jose knew, though, that he would have some questions to answer. And they came soon enough.

They finally finished the first meat-filled dinner the girls had seen since they had moved; the apartment was filled with the warmth of savory roasting juices. No longer would they be forced to subsist on cheap beans for their protein. Hilarity and horseplay between Jose, Emma and Bonnie escalated just like old times.

"Jose, why don't you take those silly glasses off? You wear them all the time. Don't you get sick of them?" Bonnie tried to swat them off as she teased him. Jose ducked, eluding her flying arms.

"Bonnie, please behave, Jose didn't come all this way to put up with your bad manners." Mama Diaz got up to give Bonnie a swat. The girls quickly settled back down under the watchful eyes of their exasperated mother, enjoying their unexpected dinner. Bonnie and Emma rose to clear the table, not needing any prompting from their mother. As the girls worked, Mama Diaz placed her hands atop Jose's.

"My boy, you are so good to us and we love you for it. But I must ask. Where is all your good fortune coming from? How can you afford to live in such homes in Florida and do all of this for us?" Jose looked deep into her confused trusting eyes. He reflected on the unwavering loving support that had saved him as a young boy, knowing no English, traumatized by the tragic deaths of his parents and being wrenched from the only home he had known in Costa Rica. It was through her efforts that part of the hole in his soul had healed. She deserved every drop of comfort his good fortune could bring to her and the girls.

"Mama, I have something important to try to explain to you. Emma . . . Bonnie, could you both come sit down?" The girls looked somber at his unexpected tone. They sat, looking at him expectantly.

"I don't know how to tell you this." Jose put his hands on top of his head in frustration and fear. "I need to tell you that I love you all very much. I would never do anything to hurt you. Do you believe me?"

"Well, yeah."

"Of course."

"My boy, what is it?" They all looked curious. Not scared yet, but he knew it would come.

"You didn't rob a bank, did you?" Emma and Bonnie cracked up, rolling their eyes comically. Jose sat silently, not knowing how to start, his tongue a leaden slab in his mouth. They stared at him with anticipation, breathless for what would clearly be a bombshell.

"You did, didn't you?" Emma whispered the accusation.

"Oh my God. He did." Bonnie clapped her hands over her mouth, amazement lighting up her face.

"No, I told you. It's not that." He took a deep breath and reached up to remove his sunglasses. Mama and the girls looked as if they had been slapped.

"*Holy shit.* What happened to your eyes?"

"Emma, watch your mouth in this house. Oh, my poor boy. What happened?" Mama, first wringing her hands and making the sign of the cross, searched her pockets for her rosaries. The brilliance of his eyes reflected into the room. He tried to remember how shocking this must look. *Should I go any further? Can they handle the whole truth? How can I avoid telling them?* Overwhelmed, he put his head down on the table, his arms burying the glow from his eyes.

"Abby and Scotty have it, too." His voice sounded hollow from inside the shelter of his arms. Mama got up from her seat to put her arms around Jose.

"My boy, does this have anything to do with your new wealth? Please tell us, Son. We're going to support you, no matter what. You know that. We're family." Her gentle supportive words felt like a balm on his young soul. He wanted desperately to lift the burden of secrecy off his inexperienced shoulders. He broke down, telling them everything. Exhaustion defeated him as he finished most of the unbelievable story. Mama got up hurriedly, putting on the teakettle. The girls looked at him with renewed interest.

"When can we meet Echo? Can we see the gold? Can I have a diamond?" The questions and silliness kept coming until Mama put an end to it.

"Girls, Jose is not on display for your pleasure. We are trying to finish our tea. Now take the ice cream out of the freezer and serve it, please."

Chastised by Mama, and not understanding the significance of Jose's revelation, the girls let up, returning to the chatter about their schoolmates and what their new house would look like. The respite allowed Jose to escape frightening the girls with any further disclosures. But he could tell Mama would not be put off so easily. Glancing at her pensive wise face, he knew she would wait for the right time to broach the subject again.

As the evening came to a close, the girls kissed him goodbye and retired to their bedroom to get ready for bed. Jose finished wiping the last dish for Mama. Folding the wet dishtowel on the rim of the sink, he announced he should be getting back to his hotel.

"I'll call Abby tonight to give her the good news. I'd like to do some shopping tomorrow if you're up to it, Mama."

"Jose, I must go to work tomorrow."

"You're never working again." Jose laughed, putting some large bills in her hands. "Call your boss, Mama, I'm taking you shopping tomorrow." She looked flustered, a big excited smile on her face.

"I can't believe our good luck." She stopped suddenly. Smoothing back the curls that fell across his forehead, Mama glanced sideways at his glowing eyes and whispered, "I hope you can find an extra minute for me tomorrow. You know you need to tell me the whole story."

Kissing her on the check, he nodded his head. "Of course, Mama, I didn't want to say any more in front of the girls. Tomorrow."

Giving her a final hug, they parted at the door. Jose skipped the dismal confining elevator, descending the stairwell down the six flights to the street. He listened to the metal thump of his shoes against the worn treads of the echoing stairwell, the walls marked with the graffiti of the current generation. He knew life in this environment gave birth to violence, drugs, various racial hatreds, rapes and casual murders. He cringed every time he thought of Abby and Scotty trying to survive in this environment as children. He hardened his determination to get Emma and Bonnie out as soon as possible.

He emerged into the sunlight, the local homies holding court on their appropriated turf at the front of the building giving him the stink eye. A few made catcalls. He thought of Mama and the girls running that gauntlet every day and he made up his mind. He would move them into his hotel for the rest of the week until they were ready to accompany him to Florida.

Hurrying back to his hotel—the same one they had stayed in when they were in Norristown, he asked to be moved into the penthouse. Short Hills was only a twenty-minute drive away. He could take the girls to school and pick them up afterwards. He began to relax, thinking the worst remained behind him.

That night Abby called, turning his plans upside down. The conversation was tight and upsetting as Jose learned she wanted him to take Mama and the girls back to Lily Pond Road. She further surprised him, confessing she knew he continued to pay the lease on the house. It wasn't that he thought that they would ever need the house again, he just didn't want there to be any unexplained discoveries when new tenants moved in. Continuing the lease prevented that. He didn't want anything unusual to be traced back to them. Just a precaution.

He fired a million questions at Abby. The fact that Abby had exposed herself to the Cobbys came as a shock. *How could she risk our security without discussing it with me?* He hadn't even known she trusted Captain Cobby enough to confide in him. When he left to find Mama and the girls, the biggest problem had been Scotty and Kane. *When did that resolve itself? And just when exactly did Abby get so chummy with Captain Cobby?* His young imagination burned with the thought of Abby spending time with the handsome Italian. *What the heck's going on?* Her unsatisfying answers left him full of doubts.

He sat in his hotel stewing over this change of events, wanting desperately to be in Sarasota to understand what Abby and Scotty were up to. He mulled over his bitter thoughts, angry about how they threatened to derail his plans for Mama Diaz and the girls. He should be celebrating, not moping around depressed about what Abby was up to.

He weighed his options. Abby wanted him to trust her and blindly ask no questions. He railed at being treated like a child. In the long run, he still had to spend time with Mama and the girls. He wanted to take them all shopping and Emma needed to complete her presentation on world extinction. She really wanted him to attend and he would. After he got them settled in Lily Pond Road again, he would hop a plane back to Florida and see for himself just what was going on.

But how to tell the girls they weren't going straight to Florida? Abby claimed she planned to bring others with her, but she wouldn't tell him why. Very ominous. He thought the emotional reveal to Mama Diaz would have to wait, the distraction in Sarasota weighing heavily on his mind.

Before he knew it, Jose's mind snapped back to the cab in Sarasota as it pulled into the driveway at Mango Lane. Paying the cab, he ran up to the front door and rang the bell. No answer. He searched his pockets for his key, slipping it into the lock. To his surprise the door popped open, unlocked all along. Odd.

He stepped into the foyer, his feet sounding a hollow tone never before noticed, as if the house didn't recognize his footstep.

"Abby? Scotty?" No one answered. He ran up the staircase to the bedroom, the bed unmade, no Abby. Returning downstairs, he headed toward the kitchen, looking around in vain, seeing no one. The dogs weren't even here. Scanning the room, he noticed the absence of Penny's big doggy bed. In its place rested a ragged old afghan, probably something Scotty had picked up for the dogs.

He stared absently at the afghan, annoyed that no one was home. Spoiling for a fight now, his eyes casually rested on the afghan's pretty turquoise color as he reminded himself they didn't know of his secret return. They thought he waited in Sussex County.

He abruptly stopped all thought, his eyes refocusing on the afghan. *What? Something about the afghan.* It drew him, an unfamiliar feeling hitting him in the solar plexus. He bent over, picking it up. Its poor condition testified to the beating it had taken over the years. He recognized the yellow maize design on the body of the afghan as a Mexican, possibly Central American design. Rubbing the afghan between his fingers, he wondered why it disturbed him.

From the front of the house he heard a racket. Stuffing the afghan under his arm, he hurried to the front door to confront an incomprehensible sight. Scotty's Jeep had pulled into the drive. Abby was out of the car directing a caravan of tractor-trailer trucks across the meticulously maintained front lawn and around the back of the house. The trucks drove over the top of their very expensive flowering bushes. *What the fuck?* He ran outside trying to flag down Abby. Unable to attract her attention, he turned to the Jeep where he found himself almost knocked over by a desperate hug from Scotty, who was accompanied a beautiful but bored, very pregnant, young black girl.

"Scotty what the heck are you guys up to? And where's Echo and the dogs?" Scotty gestured to the back of the Jeep.

"Echo's in my car. The dogs are waiting for us on the boat along with Peter and his girlfriend."

"Peter has a girlfriend? And why is everyone heading for the boat? You going somewhere?" Scotty looked uncomfortable as Jose questioned him. Feeling a quick elbow in the ribs from Kenya, he offered an introduction.

"Uh, Jose, this is Kenya McCready. She's here to help with the animals. She worked at the sanctuary."

"Hey there, chicky, you know where I can sit down?" Inadvertently ignoring the introduction, Jose grabbed Scotty's shoulders, giving him a shake.

"Sanctuary? I don't know what you're talking about. Can you help me get Abby over here?"

"Sure, uh, what are you doing with Teddy's blanket?"

"This is Teddy's? You mean it's Chloe's?"

"Yeah, it's an old baby blanket of hers. Chloe likes to use it for Ted." Jose handed the afghan to Scotty. Jose watched the blanket in Scotty's hands, distracted by Scotty directing Kenya down to the boat. Looking across the lawn, he saw Abby making her way across the yard, tears dripping down her face. Running over to Jose, she threw her arms around him, crushing him in her sweaty rumpled embrace.

"Thank God, you're here. I don't think I can do this alone anymore." Her face pressed into his shirt, muffling the sound of her crying and the tears soaking the material. "We have to get out of here." She looked up into his face, her glasses askew, exposing the fear in her eyes.

"Babe, babe, easy. What the heck's going on?"

They both turned, seeing Scotty jump into his Jeep and tear off down the road, obviously heading to Chloe's house. Abby wiped the back of her hand across her face, her words almost incoherent.

"We rescued the animals . . . forced me . . . save them . . . back to the cavern . . . Echo's help . . . millions will die . . . Cobby's help . . . didn't freak . . . to Tampa . . . elude the cops, can't have them slow us down. Gotta hurry, please Jose, *help me*." She looked down the road after the Jeep, swallowing hard, trying to catch her breath. "We have to get Scotty back here. We can't stay. The neighbors will notice. The cops will come. I need Echo if there's trouble. She's still in the back seat of the Jeep."

"Okay, okay. I still don't understand what's happening but I get the urgency. I'll go get Scotty. When I get back, we need to have a talk, Abby. Understood? You finish up here and get these trucks out of the way. Have the boat on standby. I'll be back as soon as I can. By the way, what's the big deal about these animals? What do you have, a bunch of dogs and cats?"

"You could say that," she muttered softly, her eyes closed shut as if in prayer, but not before Jose glimpsed again her raw fear.

"You okay, Abby?"

She nodded, opening her eyes to give him a solemn fragile smile. "I'm better now. I'll fill you in with the details later. Just go get Scotty. *Hurry*." She kissed him hard on the lips, then ran off around the back of the house.

Chapter 15

Scotty tested his plan, running it quickly through his head. Tearing down the road to Chloe's house, he realized he had never intended to let her perish with the rest of the unprotected population. And Echo was the one who would help him prevent it.

He screeched to a halt on the road in front of her house. He was in luck, the front gate was open and unattended. A yellow cab sat in front of the house waiting for his fare.

"Echo, I'm going to go get Chloe to come out to the car to get Teddy's blanket. I want you to implant her, okay? We better take Teddy with us or she'll never forgive me. Can't leave the little dude behind, anyway. You onboard, girl?" Luminous auras signaled assent.

Scotty took a last look at Echo who sat, cool as a cucumber, in her shades and fanny pack. "Wish me luck." Giving Echo a thumb's up, he shut the Jeep door.

Scotty quickly ran up to the front door, finding it unlatched. Looking around, he double checked he wasn't observed; the cabbie was snoozing. He soundlessly slipped in the house, his shirt stuck to his back from the heat, sweat outlining his wings.

He boldly ran through the empty foyer and up the stairs to Chloe's room, softly tapping on her door. He could hear banging and drawers being slammed. Opening the door a crack, he saw Chloe packing a suitcase, the tracks of recent tears still drying on her cheeks. She looked awful. He opened the door wider. She glanced up, instant apprehension on her face. She jumped in delight when she realized it was Scotty, bowling him over as she threw her arms around him.

"Scotty, Daddy's taking me away for a long time. He said we

can't take Teddy. I'll run away first. I'd rather die." She started to cry again, clinging to him as if he could solve her problem. *Which I can,* he thought happily.

"Chloe, come *with me.* Of course, we can take Teddy with us. I have his blanket in the truck. Grab your suitcase and let's go." He grabbed Teddy, who looked at him with his tiny bright eyes and pink tongue flicking as if he could taste the air, so laden was it with emotion. They ran down the wide hallway, Scotty carrying her suitcase, while Chloe held Teddy to her chest.

Jose jumped in his SUV after Abby ran off to supervise the animals as they boarded the boat. He wondered how she planned to keep the cats and dogs from killing each other. Oh well, he knew she would handle it in her own capable fashion. And it had better be a good one if the size of the trucks were any indication of the number of cats and dogs.

Rounding the bend in his SUV, he located Chloe's house. Along the road across from the house sat Scotty's Jeep. Parking on the other side of the road, he crossed over to it. Peering through the open windows he saw Echo in the back seat with Teddy's blanket. He ran to Echo's side of the car, feeling the heat inside as he removed Echo's sunglasses. His mind's eye registered the aura as Echo complained about the loss of her sunglasses.

"I want to be a dude, Brother Jose. I need my shades. Brother Scotty said I am cool."

This was not the time for Echo to turn into a child on him. "Come here, you nut. You can be a dude later. I need to get you out of that hot car." He lifted Echo out of the Jeep which was heating up unmercifully, even with the windows down. He looked around to find a safe spot for Echo while he went into the house to get Scotty. Nothing. *She'll just have to come with me. What's the difference anyway? According to Abby we're going on the lam anyway.*

Grabbing Teddy's blanket, Jose walked past a sleeping cabbie and up to the front door, finding it cracked open. He rang the bell, surprised to see no one around. According to Scotty, the house was full of guards and other staff. Holding Echo in his arms, he pushed the door open wider and walked in.

Looking around the sumptuous foyer he wondered where to start looking first. Turning to the right, he walked through the opening to a huge room dominated by a mammoth stone fireplace. Empty. Softly calling out to Scotty, he stopped to listen. The house remained silent.

Moving on, he reflected on the tastefully expensive appointments lushly decorating the mansion. There was a time when he would have been intimidated by the wealth represented here. He would have longed for it himself. Looking around, he saw no sign of real life in the room. No signs of a real family. Just cold show pieces. Now that lady luck had chosen to allow them to experience such grandeur themselves, it left him unsatisfied. The only achievement that mattered to him was a healthy, happy family. That's what he ached for. He could be happy anywhere if his loved ones were with him.

Leaving the living room, Jose found himself in a light, bright space containing a lot of plants and wicker furniture, along with three ornamental freestanding cages. Peering inside he saw the monkeys Scotty had mentioned. They appeared timid and fragile, obviously on the older side, their muzzles tinged with gray, their skin thinning. Surprisingly, he knew the two on the left were howler monkeys. He also knew they originated from Costa Rica, his birthplace. He backed away from the monkey cages, Echo suddenly heavy in his arms. He set her down on the floor, feeling dizzy.

A taunting voice suddenly pierced the silence, seeming to come from an adjoining room. The voice sounded rich, commanding, and familiar. *Very* familiar. His head swam with confusion as he took Echo's hand and walked toward the voice dumbfounded, disbelieving the déjà vu threatening to drown him.

Jose blindly stepped through the door to confront the tall,

aristocratic man who stood castigating a middle-aged handsome man on the floor by the body of an older woman. But Jose comprehended little. His head reeled with the shock of recognition. The younger man was Omar Nasir, the Socialist New World nominee for the position of President of the United States.

They noticed his presence. Nasir used the opportunity to try to rise off the floor, only to be kicked in the head by the tall man's heavy leather riding boots, an affectation that Jose remembered well.

"Senor Brooks . . . my God," Jose whispered, confusion rendering him almost speechless. Brooks squinted at him.

"Do I know you, young man?" His tone rang with dismissive impatience.

"I am Jose. You were my friend. I . . . don't understand. What are you doing here?" In a long overdue flash, he made a connection. "The monkeys, they're yours. I know them. I played with them as a boy in Costa Rica. You took care of me when . . ." His voice trailed off as confusion got the best of him.

"He's not your friend, kid. He's just an everyday kidnapper and murderer."

Jose looked from one to the other. But Omar wasn't finished. He was shouting, "Who do you think kidnapped your infant sister?"

Brooks reached over to spit on Omar, imperious disdain and contempt scrawled across his aged face.

Scotty and Chloe emerged from the mansion, not seeing a soul. They tossed Teddy and the suitcase in the back seat. Just as Scotty started the car, he turned around to scan the back seat. Echo was gone. Looking around wildly, he recognized Jose's SUV on the other side of the road.

"Oh no. I have to go back in the house. That's Jose's truck. He must have come after me. And Echo's missing."

"Echo? You brought your cat?"

"Yeah, and sorry, she's definitely not a cat. I can't leave without her. You stay here with Teddy. Keep the air on." He dashed back to the front door, letting himself in again, listening carefully, hoping to hear where Jose might have gone. Echo had probably seen him pull up to the house and, for some reason, followed him in. From the foyer, the silence bounced off the walls making his skin itch with nervousness. Making his way slowly to the back of the house, he crept cautiously, afraid that if he got caught, he would lose his chance to save Chloe. He jumped, knocking off his sunglasses as he felt a hand on his shoulder.

"No Echo yet? Oh gee, there's those eyes of yours."

"Chloe, damn it, you scared me." There she stood with Teddy in her arms. "I want you to stay in the car. You'll be safer there. Please go back to the truck."

"I can help you find Echo. We can get out of here quicker. I know my dad will be looking for me soon. The cab out front must be for him. I don't know where everyone is. This is pretty weird." Suddenly, they heard voices from the back of the house.

"You have to stay here. I'll go see if I can find Jose. Echo must be with him." He moved quickly to the back of the house, passing by the monkey cages to Chloe's father's study, where he was stunned to find Jose grasping Echo's hand while Chloe's uncle held a gun to the head of a man sitting on the floor, surrounded by paper money. Paper money that didn't quite cover the dead body of Chloe's old nanny, Mrs. Elbarad.

"Daddy?" Jose turned his back on the two men to see Scotty and Chloe standing at the doorway behind him. Jose turned back to Brooks, with one thing on his mind.

"Why would you kidnap my sister? You were our friend. Papa . . . my mama . . ." Jose held Teddy's blanket in front of his face, the horror fully dawning. "Oh my God, no . . . this was made by my mama. It was wrapped around my baby sister when she was kidnapped. How . . . ?" He slowly turned to Chloe, tears flowing.

"Chloe? Omar Nasir is your father?"

"Yes, what's going on, Daddy? Uncle Brooks, what are you doing?" Confusion evident, she backed away as if to escape the sinister sight, incomprehensible facts unraveling in front of her. "Daddy, what's happening? How do you know Scotty's brother? Why are you saying all of these horrible things about Uncle Brooks?" She seemed to finally see the gun in Andrew Brooks' hand and the body on the floor. "*Mrs. Elbarad, oh, my gosh.*"

"Chloe, you know you're my baby girl." Omar pleaded from the floor, his hand stretched out to her.

They were all surprised when the shot came. The noise was paralyzing, and everyone froze in place as the ramifications left them speechless. Omar Nasir, the Presidential hope of the Socialist New World Party, lay in a pool of blood, his gelatinous brain matter plastered all over the artfully marbleized salmon walls behind him. Scotty reached out in shock, grabbing Chloe, who stood hyperventilating. Crushing her to his chest he instructed her to breathe.

Jose tried to bring himself under control. He needed time to think. Brooks still held a gun on them. He looked directly at Brooks in confusion.

"You killed my parents, kidnapped my baby sister for Mr. Nasir? And then you shoot him? He was going to be President. Why? Why . . . all of this? Why did you have to kill my papa, my mama?" His voice sank again with the enormity of the dead bodies lying on the floor. Things from his childhood flashed back to him. After the murders, the empty monkey cages, his constant grogginess, the infant cries on the airplane taking him to the United States. "You drugged me." He was astonished, but it explained so much. Well planned and well funded.

"Omar Nasir? You could almost say he works *for me*. I answer to Mohammed al Qua Terique of the Salafis. We owned Omar Nasir." He said it so proudly, the light of a madman gleaming from his bulging eyes. He gave them a long look.

"Jose and young Chloe. Ha. You both need to get over yourselves. You were just necessary pawns, needed in our efforts to package Omar for the stupid American public. Omar's wife cracked up after the death of their baby. A real nut job. Unstable and unreliable. We were forced to keep her hidden away until she snapped out of it. We tried a few methods of self-medication ourselves. Nothing worked. After a while, we realized the only thing that might work was another baby. Unfortunately, she could no longer carry a child. So we concocted a fabulous idea. Don't blame *me*. What else were we to do?

"Chloe fit our requirements perfectly. Your mother contracted polio while she was pregnant with Chloe, giving her the immunities she would need to avoid the disease herself. We went to great lengths to make it happen, as you know. The only reason you were not killed along with your parents was because I had taken a shine to you. You loved my little monkeys. No one knew I had not killed you. I think I went over and above what anyone would have done. Didn't I find a nice home for you? I kept my eye on you as long as I could. I had to disappear eventually, hoping to avoid the very kind of thing that has just happened. You could have unraveled everything. I guess I have no one to blame but myself. What an unwelcome coincidence to find you here. Coming back to bite me in the ass, eh? But we did find the perfect infant to lure Mrs. Nasir out of her depression. We had the perfect picture of the happy youthful political family, just what we needed to seduce the stupid American public."

Senor Brooks took a long hard look at Jose. He stared right back, hatred flaming his eyes through his sunglasses. Senor Brooks exhaled, a long sigh sputtered from his throat. "If it makes any difference, I have grown quite fond of Chloe. But not that little rat of hers. *Goddamn dog*. Sorry to say that our plans have changed. The house staff is long gone, their planes taking them to safety. Sorry I can't extend the same opportunity to all of you. The little rat will be the first to go." So saying, he raised his gun and took a shot at Teddy who stood unprotected on the floor. The little dog collapsed, and Chloe screamed hysterically, her arms flailing in the air out of control.

Turning to Scotty, Brooks motioned to Chloe.

"Do you mind shutting her up?" Brooks suddenly noticed Echo watching from behind Jose's legs. Extending his gun hand, he pointed with it. "What in the hell do you have there? Send that little thing over to me." Leaning down, Jose whispered hurriedly to Echo.

"Echo, that is a very bad human, he wants to hurt us." His mind aura turned turgid.

"I cannot let that happen, Brother Jose."

"That's enough talking there. Send the creature over to me *now*."

As Echo walked haltingly toward Brooks, her crystal antlers split open, sending her mysterious emulsion to hit Brooks smack in the face.

"*What the fuck . . .?*" His voice gurgled as the emulsion ate into his skin, taking it down to the bone, eating everything, even his clothes. The gun fell from his hand as his fingers disappeared. As his skeleton teetered, the emulsion disappeared back into Echo's antlers as fast as it had arrived, the crystal seamlessly sealing back up. The skeleton crashed to the floor, breaking the spell that had held them in its thrall.

"*Holy shit*. We've got to get out of here." Jose turned to run. "What's the matter with Chloe?" She was lying on the floor in a fetal position, Teddy at her side, blood running out of his little body, pooling under them. Teddy's pupils were fixed, Chloe's glazed and unfocused. Scotty knelt at her side, feeling for her pulse. Panicking, he screamed for Echo, who already had her tail in the air sending out her healing to Teddy.

"We have to go, Scotty. Let me take her. You grab Echo and Teddy."

"No, I'll take Chloe, Echo needs to heal her." He pushed Jose away, gagging on the smell of sulfur.

"Stop. *This is my sister*. You know it's forbidden for Echo to heal more people. Chloe's just fainted." As Jose's voice broke, Scotty backed away allowing Jose to scoop up his sister. They ran to the next room where the monkeys stood at the front of their cages, mouths agape, tiny hands gripping the bars to see what was happening. Jose glanced away.

Running to the SUV, he slid her onto the back seat, then belted her in. Scotty lifted Teddy and Echo into the Jeep, having first deposited Chloe's suitcase on the front seat. Teddy appeared dazed but on the road to recovery.

"Watch Chloe, I'll be right back." Crossing the road, he ran over to the Jeep. "I need you, girl." Echo stood up and jumped into Jose's arms. Together they ran back to the mansion. It only took a few minutes before they were back outside, the elderly monkeys following, recipients of Echo's implants. They calmly but quickly leaped into the back of Scotty's Jeep, sitting quietly like a group of little wise men, their diminutive fingers busy grooming to keep themselves soothed.

"I couldn't leave them behind. They're innocent." Jose started his SUV while Scotty ran back to his Jeep. Hurrying home with Chloe on the backseat, Jose wondered if the obvious evacuation of the guards and staff at the Nasir mansion had anything to do with the flight from Sarasota that Abby was planning. Clearly, something bad was going to happen, he just didn't know when. He thanked God that he had decided to come back to Florida instead of waiting for Abby on Lily Pond Road. That decision had, astonishingly, brought his sister back into his life. He wiped his hands across his eyes, his tears hot, his eyes swollen. He wanted to scream at the top of his lungs to relieve his overwhelming feelings of impotence. He wanted to punish the selfish psychopaths himself. He wept painfully with the knowledge of how his family had been used in such a brutal and monstrous fashion.

He watched the monkeys in the rearview mirror. They had saved his life in Costa Rica. The least he could do was return the favor.

He would take them on the yacht with Abby's cats and dogs. Maybe they would help him recover from the shock of this savage revelation. At the worst, the monkeys would remind him of the small satisfaction he had got watching Andrew Brooks' self-satisfied smug face as it disintegrated in front of him.

Chapter 16

The suburban Dallas landscape reveled in the hot and dusty weather—just what the suburbanites expected every day. Joe wouldn't actually call it suburbia though. There was not a house in sight for ten miles. His gritty tired blue eyes looked down the road seeing just raw dust and scrub. Hot and dusty didn't quite cover it either. Try roasting and scorching. He lifted his sweat-soaked ten gallon off his pounding noggin, wiping his forehead with the back of his sleeve. He could feel dust collecting in the crevices of his clean-cut athletic features. He spat on the hard-packed clay under his feet, feeling the grit on his teeth. Behind him, he could smell the heat radiating off the hot tarmac, creating shimmering windows which blocked his view of the line of private planes along the side of the hanger.

He glanced at his watch, seeing his new employer was ten minutes late. Nothing to get his dander up about as Jenny would tell him. She had made great strides with him since the baby had been born. She really knew how to create a relaxed and harmonious ambience in their gracious Dallas village home. It was for the baby, of course. But it helped him relax too. He smiled to himself, as he realized the strides he had made in his ability to manage his stress had come directly from Jenny and the baby. He was sorry they hadn't started a family as soon as they were married.

Their first serious meeting had occurred on a long layover in Buffalo, New York where they had been snowed in due to a winter storm heading toward the frigid town. As part of the flight crew, the pilots had all been invited to an impromptu party in a suite the flight attendants had located. He and his co-pilot had decided to attend, even though he usually avoided such events. Not because he wasn't interested. It was just that as one of the few single pilots in the fleet, he was always a target for husband-hunting flight attendants. He preferred to date back home in Dallas.

He had noticed Jenny once before on another flight, but they hadn't had the opportunity to talk. Her pretty feminine face was something he would have been attracted to anyway, but he had been charmed to find she was a woman with varied interests beyond her job. That meant no shop talk for her, another bonus in his book. Joe and Jenny. It hadn't taken long.

The baby had come three years after they were married. Jenny left her job to become a full-time mother. That meant he needed to pick up the slack with some freelance flying on the side. A pilot for hire on short-term jobs, just the puddle jumpers. His schedule was flexible enough that he had been able to fit in a couple jobs per month, without any effect on his responsibility to his airline.

He had been contacted for this flight through his online ad on an aviation site. It had turned out to be a good source of business for him. He glanced at his watch again. Now they were twenty minutes late. He knew he was overly punctual. He had to be. But he felt surprised that they were late. His plan consisted of flying an executive and some trade show supplies to Vegas for a convention. Eyeballing the small planes on the tarmac through the heat shimmers, he didn't see anything he thought suitable for his executive. Except for the light jet on the end, by itself. A Citation CJ4. A little fancy for a remote little airport like this, and he didn't think they would use anything that big for one man and a couple of cardboard boxes of brochures.

The searing heat beat down, sucking his energy, leaving behind a tired and flagging spirit. The client had specifically asked that he wait outside the shack that served as the cool spot for filing flight plans. *Damn.* He hoped he wasn't getting stood up. He pulled out his cellphone, checking the dial. Nothing there. Well, at least he had their deposit.

A faint rumble intruded on his thoughts. He looked down the road to see a plain white delivery van approach, coated in road dust. He didn't really expect the van to be his executive. In his experience, they liked to travel in style. Limos and private drivers. Especially executives who could afford to travel in private jets, even if they were only hired for the moment.

He watched the two men from the truck walk toward him. They both looked dark skinned, faintly Middle Eastern. Their clothes were ordinary to shabby. Not what he expected. A faint tingle of alarm sounded in the back of his head. Everyone knew to be suspicious of middle eastern types around aircraft these days. He dismissed his concern as overly suspicious. What would be the odds? Nothing abnormal had ever happened to him in his thirty eight years of life.

"You Joseph Lansing?" The tall one held out his hand. "I am Abdul Ahad. I am pleased to meet you. This is my associate, Tarek." Joe shook hands with them both. Tarek said nothing. Abdul seemed to be in a state. Joe could see sweat beading on his forehead as fast as the heat sucked it away. *Is the man sick?*

"You okay there, Abdul?" He glanced with concern at Tarek who punched Abdul in the arm and mumbled some Arab words to him. They must have helped because he straightened up and gave a quick weak smile. Joe's tingle of alarm grew stronger. *Nah, I must be watching too much television.*

"Captain Lansing, I would first like to show you what you will be flying." Tarek motioned with his hand to the end of the runway and the Citation. Together they strolled toward the jet, while Abdul peeled off to bring up the van. As the van passed them, Jose noticed it seemed to be riding low on its shocks.

"So, Tarek, you're my passenger?"

"No, Captain. Abdul is your passenger." They had reached the Citation as the white van pulled up to the jet for unloading.

"Now hold on there, Tarek. My understanding is I'll be flying a corporate executive to Vegas for a convention. Seems there's a small misunderstanding here." His tingle had now turned into a jackhammer and he knew he had to get out of there.

"No misunderstanding, Captain." Tarek smoothly extracted a handgun from underneath his loose cotton shirt. "You are flying to Las Vegas, Nevada. Home to the hedonistic capitalistic western devils. My friend Abdul is more than a stupid western executive. He is a martyr for his homeland, his family and his religion."

Oh, shit, are you kidding me? His bowels took a hit as they loosened. "Hey, hey, buddy. This isn't my fight. I've got a family, a brand new baby."

"*Shut up.*" Tarek raked Joe with the butt of his handgun, the warm metal leaving a gash across the side of his temple to his eyebrow. The blood flowed heavily down his face. On a signal from Tarek, Abdul opened the back of the van, releasing three other men who began pulling something to the edge of the tailpipe. They left it resting there while they released the hatch and pulled down the storage door to the jet. Joe could not make out what the object was, but he had a pretty good idea.

"*You can't make me do this.*" Joe's brave words didn't even merit a comment. He was yanked back and dragged to the rear of the van where they knocked him to the ground and kicked him repeatedly. Pulling him up, he had difficulty breathing. His ribs felt busted where the more vicious kicks had landed. His head was pounding from his contusions and the heat made his injuries feel ten times more painful.

Tarek grabbed a fistful of his thick black hair, yanking his head back. The sun beat down unmercifully on his bloody face. He glanced to the side, noticing that Tarek had something in his hand.

"Let me show you what a good photographer Abdul is." He thrust a photograph in Joe's face. Joe squinted, vainly trying to make out the figures in the photo. As the blood cleared from his eye, he saw one of the men from the van holding a tiny baby in his arms, facing the camera and smiling. In the background he could clearly see the form of a bald woman making love to a man. No, her hands were tied and being held by another man. *She was being raped. God no, please.* He could make out the feminine features of his Jenny's face as she lay screaming, her mouth opened wide while the man atop raped her. And her hair, what—? He squinted. It looked like her hair had been yanked out by the roots; blood and clumps of hair littered the floor around her head.

"What a lovely baby boy you have, Captain. If you would like him to remain a boy, you will cooperate. Let us commence with our preflight checklist. Are we on the same page now?"

Joe barely heard what the man had said. He knew his life was over. Tears slipped from his eyes at the thought of them hurting their baby. And Jenny. He wondered if she was still alive. His knees buckled, crashing him to the ground. They pulled him to his feet.

"I think the Captain needs a little incentive." Tarek held out his hand. One of the men slapped a cellphone in his palm. Looking at the dial he pressed a number and held it to his ear, then gave an order in Arabic. The phone was then held up to Joe's ear. He could hear an infant screaming in the background. Then Jenny.

"*Joe, they have the baby. Do what they want. Please Joe. They have the baby.*" She sounded hysterical.

"Well, Captain, shall we begin?" Tarek snapped the cellphone closed. Feeling like a zombie, Joe allowed himself to be led to the cockpit. He was on autopilot, going through the motions. In his numbed state, one thing was clear to him. He would not survive this. Nor would his family. He wiped away bitter tears, trying to think of the love he and Jenny had been lucky enough to share, if only for a while. That was all you had on this Earth. A while.

He looked over to the man guarding him as he moved around in the cockpit, readying his flight. He glanced back to the lounge and saw Tarek hand a gun to Abdul. He could see from the cockpit that whatever had been on the van was now stowed away in the belly of the jet. He looked away as Tarek came forward. The Arab nodded to the man guarding him, instructing him to leave the cockpit.

"Your wife and child will be released once this flight has reached its destination. I do not want you disturbed by the images of what will happen to your wife and child if this plane does not arrive in Las Vegas. My disappointment will be swift. Abdul will be left onboard to guide you. He is a simple man with a simple task. But you are not to underestimate his determination to martyr himself. Are we clear?"

Joe stared at the man holding the gun on him, wondering what kind of life he must lead to be able to do this to an innocent family. *Or is he just insane?*

"I asked you if all is clear to you. Did you not hear me?" The gun was at his throat, painfully pressed against his Adam's apple.

"Yes, yes, I understand." His movements seemed to be in slow motion as he fastened himself in. Clearly there was to be no flight plan filed. He wondered if the airport would alert the authorities.

"A flight plan was filed for you this morning. We could not take the chance with you, now could we? And yes, I realize you have probably guessed our cargo, but fear not. You are not the only one. Another plane will take off two hours after you, for another destination. It is headed for New York City. We know the plane will never get close enough to the city to do any damage so we plan to offload to a waiting truck. The authorities will be so busy with the results of your little excursion that they will be too busy to check all of the small little ways one can penetrate the defensive line of such a big city. But we will not be suspected this time. The Pakistani government will be blamed. On instruction from China and Russia, of course. Everyone knows how Pakistan betrays the U.S. as it sucks away at your taxpayers' money. And you know the Israelis will have to respond when their wounded devil cousin demands retribution.

"Can you see the delightful possibilities?" His face shined, greasy with religious fervor, demonic malevolence making his eyes glitter. Joe looked away, wanting to be sick, wishing he could die now. He had no reason to live with his family in their hands. His life was done.

Leaning over his seat, he vomited. Tarek looked down, seeing the vomit splash his socks and his sandals. He glared in disgust.

"What do you expect?" Wiping his mouth on the tail of his shirt, Joe fatalistically turned back to his gauges. "What if I told you I'm too sick to fly?"

"I would have to call my associates keeping company with your wife and baby. I would then have to ask them if they were feeling too sick to do their jobs. What do you think they might say?"

Joe decided to keep his mouth shut. He rubbed his stomach, hoping it would settle down. There was nothing he could do or say to change what was going to happen. Everything that mattered to him had been viciously snatched away. He stared blankly out the windshield, feeling venom in his blood. Nothing he could do? Nothing . . .? He shut his eyes for a second then took a deep breath. *These scum fuckers haven't heard the last of Mama Lansing's oldest boy Joe. Not by a long shot . . .*

Chapter 17

Kenya McCready tried unsuccessfully to make herself comfortable in Captain Cobby's stateroom. Pregnancy sure brought out the chivalry in a man. Even though he had kindly insisted she rest in his own cabin, she still could not rid herself of the conflicting smells of salt water, wet fur, dung and fish. This was definitely *not* her idea of a cushy break from the sanctuary. She rubbed her expanding middle reflexively. Sauntering over to the side of the room, she opened the porthole in case she needed to vomit. Her stomach rebelled, queasy from the slight rocking motion of the yacht. *Yeah, the yacht's the real deal.* She wished the girls back at the home could see her here. But without the animals. *And the smells.* Maybe with an icy margarita, some jive-ass tunes and one or two sizzling hot, fine pieces of dude flesh to hang on her every gesture.

An hour ago, she had stood at the side of the extra-wide metal gangplank attached from the dock to the yacht. The animals had placidly trudged over the gangplank. Terrified to cut in line, especially when the camels started to board, she had decided she would happily wait her turn, preferring to evade the brunt of their wicked kicks.

The craziest thing had been the cats: the lions and the tigers. They had chuffed, unusually alert, heads moving like metronomes, slowly taking stock of their surroundings. Yet they had showed no reaction to the unusual situation. They had single-mindedly padded onboard, deliberately taking their time. No fighting. Not even a quick spat with a kennel mate.

She had thought it looked like a contrived scene from a movie. As she had marveled at the behavior of the cats, she had seen two men working furiously inside the yacht directing the animals where to go once they had made it onboard. The cats, bears and the ungulates had made themselves comfortable on the large, slippery fiberglass deck. The camels had settled down nicely, looking very comfortable, sitting with their legs tucked under their big brown bodies. Their curly heads had swayed this way and that, long batting eyelashes above expressive eyes which missed nothing.

The bears, all eight of them, had taken up more than their share of room at the bow of the yacht. Massive furry craniums had rested on commodious haunches to create a seamless clique.

Her attention had veered to the back of the line where Abby stood, trying to hurry along the herd of goats. She had motioned to Kenya, waving her over.

"I need Captain Cobby and his son Kane. Go onboard and find them for me, please. I need them to help me with the turtles. Go ahead now."

Kenya had eyed the gangplank. The goats had reached the yacht and boarded, funneling to the deck next to the cats. *Oh boy.* She had winced as they settled down next to the felines. The gangplank had been almost clear. A troop of ring-tail lemurs, after prancing their way across the lawn, had joined her as she took her turn on the gangplank.

"Captain Cobby? Captain?" Kenya had waved her hand in the air as the two men had looked up, watching her waddle onto the yacht, all long caramel legs and belly. "Oh, Captain Cobby, Abby needs you. You too, chicky." Eyeing Kane, she had placed her hand on her back to support her spine. "Something about the turtles. She probably needs help lifting them."

"Miss, you look like you could use a place to lie down." The captain had taken her arm, unexpectedly directing her through the salon to the cabins. He had opened the first door they had come to. "Take mine, it'll be safe for you here." Clearly trying to get her out of the way, he had smiled charmingly, then closed the door with her safely inside.

Yeah, inside with all the rocking and the disgusting smells. Fuming, she paced the small room, missing all the action. She fingered a golden hoop dangling from her ear. *What about the hunk of hotness who appears to be the captain's son?* Maybe this little jaunt wouldn't be all work, after all. If she didn't get out of this cabin, she wouldn't be meeting anyone. She wondered what had happened to Abby's brother, Scotty. Yeah, two hot guys who could be at her beck and call. Excitement at the juicy opportunity made her bold.

Turning to the stateroom door, she cracked it open, finding no one about. Listening, she could hear banging from above.

Cautiously, she crept across the salon to the stairs, side-stepping a troop of elderly monkeys. She glanced down at her foot, her sneaker landing on something squishy. She wrinkled her nose and wiped it on the side of the steps. *Ah, why bother. It's not like it won't happen again.* Slowly, she ascended the stairs, peering around the deck. The coast was clear. She scampered back toward the gangplank in time to see everyone rushing across the yard to the yacht.

The strange man she had met on their arrival held a young girl in his arms. *Jose,* she remembered. He was crying. Scotty ran alongside them with his funky little pet on his hip. *Is he crying too?* The captain's son carried a Louis Vuitton suitcase, *probably a fake,* she sniffed. Abby and the captain shouted to get out of the way, manhandling a large thirty-five-pound wood tortoise between them. She backed up against the railing, quickly removing herself from their path.

The sound of a gruff broken motor drew her attention to the ground behind the procession. Bringing up the rear, an overlooked tiny brown dog tried to keep up. He looked like a long-haired toy poodle with a turned-up nose. She could hardly make out his features. He just looked like an entirely curly brown mop head. Brown eyes without any white, brown drop of a nose, barely discernible brown lips. *Except for his teeth,* she realized, as he grimaced comically up at her. *Itty bitty white chicklets.* He looked like a baby werewolf. As the crowd rushed past her, she scooped him up. He snuggled up on her shoulder against her neck, just like he belonged there. Flicking his teeny pink tongue out, he licked her cheek, a quick thank you. *Yes, I do have that effect on men and boys.* Giving the little dog a soft kiss, she carried him back down into the salon where all the action was congregating.

The salon reeked with noise and hot smells. Jose placed the young girl on the sofa where she lay unconscious. Abby and the captain clambered down the stairs after having secured the turtle. Jose started yelling at Abby.

"What the hell is going on here? These are the cats you told me about? *Are you kidding me?* And I guess you just forgot to mention the bears?" Kenya decided to find a quiet seat in the corner where she could sort out who was who. Looking past Abby to the doorway, she saw a man and woman enter the salon. A child trailed behind them. *Holy Christ.* It looked as if they had been beaten. She knew exactly what those bruises meant. Bracing the little brown dog still perched comfortably on her shoulder, she took a seat at the granite table near the galley and tuned in, trying to make sense of all the shouting voices.

"I told you we have cats." Abby turned away to open a door which let out a deluge of dogs. A liver and white springer spaniel, a small skunky looking Shih Tzu, and a pumped up curly-haired, white mutt which ran over to Abby's brother, jumping up on his leg. The funny little creature he called his pet flew out of Scotty's arms to land on the back of the white dog's neck, where he perched, wrapping his skinny leathery arms around the dog as if it was his long lost buddy. Scotty spoke from the sofa where he sat holding the young girl's hand.

"They're not dangerous. Echo implanted them. They do exactly what we want them to do. We had to save them, Jose. Can we worry about the cats later? What about Chloe?"

Abby's cute brother was mighty concerned about the girl on the sofa. A colorful macaw abruptly flew into the salon, touching down atop the stainless steel refrigerator next to her. She carefully opened the refrigerator, juggling the little brown dog on her shoulder. Scanning the shelves, she grabbed an apple. Removing a knife from the drawer at the sink, she sliced into the apple, handing a piece to the macaw. The brilliantly feathered creature took it in his claw and made himself busy eating, as if he knew all along that refrigerators were for perching on and copping fresh goodies. Turning back to the crowded salon, she saw everyone staring at her.

"Hey, chickies." She gave a cute little salute and took her seat at the table. She felt the pointed stare of the moon-faced guy who had entered with the beaten woman and child. She thought the woman could be pretty if she didn't have the cut down the side of her face, ending with a poorly stitched lip. The man's round bespectacled face bore into her own; telegraphing suspicious hostility. *Hey, what'd I do?* The dorky guy turned his back to her, opening his mouth to speak as the captain pushed him aside.

"We're all loaded. The trucks are on their way to Tampa. They'll meet us at the dock. I think it would help if everyone sat down and we filled them in on the plan. We need to get organized down here so I can cast off. Everyone here is going?"

Kenya sprang up out of her chair.

"*Hey*, I'm not going anywhere. You have to let me off and take me back. I got responsibilities, ya know."

Abby raised her hand at Kenya. "Give me a minute, will you? I'll let you make up your own mind about what you want to do. Although I would prefer that you decide to come with us. That's an invitation, of course." She lowered her hand, turning back to the crowd in the salon.

"Why did you bring Chloe onboard? Is she sick?"

Scotty started to speak the same time as Jose, who still shed silent tears. "I tried to tell you. Chloe is my sister."

Abby looked skeptical at Jose's words.

"What—?"

"Please, just listen to me. We've been through *hell*. Did you know Chloe's father turned out to be Omar Nasir? Her Uncle Brooks was the same Senor Brooks who orchestrated my adoption to the Diaz family. Those monkeys over there are his." He pointed to the elderly troop that had made themselves comfortable all over the elegant sideboard near Kenya. "Remember Scotty telling us about them? Well, they're the very same monkeys that lived down the street from my house when I was a boy and my parents were murdered. The whole thing was some kind of a plot to steal a baby for Nasir's wife. *Chloe is my baby sister. They stole her and murdered my parents.*" Jose broke down, cradling the young girl in his arms, his tears dripping down into her hair.

"*My God.*" Abby and Scotty looked shocked to the core. The captain and his son looked uneasy, Captain Cobby's face draining of color.

"This is Omar Nasir's daughter? Kane, you must have known that. They've lived on the island for years. Why didn't you say something?"

"Dad, Chloe is younger than me so I never paid that much attention. It's not like I hung out with her until Scotty started to date her. I didn't grow up around here like everyone else, remember?" The bitterness in his voice caught Kenya's ear. She stood up, clapping her hands over the din.

"We've got to call the cops. No, the newspapers. This is big." Kenya whipped out her cellphone, looking over to Abby with raised eyebrows.

"No, Kenya, the police can't do anything. They're all dead. They're dead." Jose wept, blubbering through his tears as Abby held his hand.

"Baby, tell me what happened. Who's dead?" Abby looked back

up at her brother. "Scotty, what happened?"

Without warning, Abby, Scotty and Jose froze, then turned to the funny little creature with the fanny pack and shades. They appeared to be waiting for the little guy to talk to them.

"What bad man, Echo?" They continued looking at the creature. Abby suddenly made a fist and brought it to her mouth. "*Oh my God. Echo killed him?*" She turned back to her brother.

"Yeah. Looks like Chloe's uncle killed Mrs. Elbarad, too. We saw him shoot Chloe's father."

"*He wasn't her father.*" The bitterness in Jose's voice brought their attention back to the young girl. Kenya was just beginning to realize Abby's brother might be involved with her. Chloe. She watched as he stroked her hair, her head lying motionless on Jose's lap. *Hmmm, the girl must be a little older than I first thought. But what was that action with the creature? Oh yeah, that's right. Her name's Echo. I'm sure Abby was talking to the creature. Echo. And it seemed like Echo gave her an answer right back.* She was starting to get nervous. *Just what the fuck's happening here?*

"Uh, Abby?" She stood and waved her hand to get Abby's attention. She started to squirm with everyone's attention on her. "I think I should go now." She plastered a great big smile on her face, feeling her facial muscles rebel. "I think you can handle everything from here, so I'll just say goodbye." Edging to the stairs, she backed up as she spoke.

"Peter, can you handle Miss McCready for me, please? She must need to lie down by now." Nodding at Kenya's obvious condition, Abby pointed toward the cabins.

"No, no, that's okay, I feel fine." Kenya kept the smile beaming as the dorky guy with the specs attempted to maneuver her to the cabin hallway. He shoved her through the door to one of the smaller cabins, isolating her from everyone.

"Kenya dear, would you please have a seat?"

She shot him an imperious evil eye. Peter the dork couldn't have sounded any more patronizing if he tried. "Don't think so, chicky. Either you let me out of here, or I'm calling my lawyer. By the way, what's with everyone wearing the stupid wraparound shades? Not cool at all. Did you see them on the weird-oh pet of Scott's?"

"I *am* a lawyer. They have eye infections. Now sit down."

She could see his temper start to sizzle beneath his oh so prissy manners. His face looked like it had been dipped in blanched putty, all saggy and stiff. Almost like he had lost the ability to show expression. Weird dude.

"That's better. So where do you live?"

"What's it to you?" She perched carefully on the edge of the only chair in the cramped room. Taking her time, she primly smoothed her white shorts, crossing her shapely legs as if she were waiting for her royal escort to arrive to sweep her away to the ball.

"Quite the prima donna, aren't you?" He sat with his head cocked, as if listening for something. Just as she was going to let him have it, she heard a noise which could only mean the engines were starting. The yacht slowly glided away from the dock. She saw the shore diminishing through the porthole to Peter's left.

"Oh no, you don't." She bounced up out of the chair before he could stop her, swinging open the cabin door, prepared to give Abby a very unflattering piece of her mind. She stopped dead as if she had been struck by a lightning bolt. Her eyes beheld a glowing brilliance—*was it gold? No, it was all different colors*—generating from Abby, Jose and Scott's eyes. She backed up, smacking into Peter as he emerged from the hallway. Pushing her aside he sat down next to the child, who appeared to belong to the woman with the gruesome lip. Without commenting, he spoke softly to Abby, who, along with Jose and her brother, had removed their shades to light up the room. Dumbfounded, she collapsed on the floor, finally speechless. Her mind raced, her flight or fight instinct engaged, honed by all the years she had taken care of herself. She was finding it near impossible to accept that the incandescent colors were coming from their eyes. She scanned the room, her gaze landing on Scott's pet, Echo, as she observed it removing its ridiculous sunglasses to expose the same luminous eyes. *What the heck?*

She couldn't move even if she wanted to. Her heart hammered in her throat, saliva turning to chalky mud in her mouth. Her muscles chattered so hard she could hear them. *Oh, God, please save me from the monsters. I promise to be a good girl from now on. Well—I mean at least for the next five years or so.*

Finding her voice, she croaked, "May I pretty please go home now?" Her croaking trailed off to a forlorn hopeless whisper. Abby slowly walked toward her, lustrous orbs zeroing in on her like a female king cobra assessing her afternoon snack. She slowly unbuttoned her blouse as Kenya tried to melt into the polished teak floor.

"You're not going to eat me now, are you?" She leaned back as far as she could.

"No, we're going to wait until you ripen up a little more."

Looking up at Abby, she felt her face drain of blood.

"Got'cha—chicky." Abby doubled over, laughing. Scott joined her with a half-hearted chuckle. The tension receded.

"Was that really necessary, babe? Don't we have enough to handle without making things worse? You okay, young lady?" Jose's small kindness started the waterworks. She was pregnant, after all. She told herself she hadn't been frightened anyway. *Hormones, remember?* She squinted up at Abby, speculation getting the best of her.

"Don'cha think that was a little mean?"

"Come on, that was a good one. I just couldn't resist. I've been under extreme stress for a while now, I just needed a little comic relief. And I don't even *have* a sense of humor. Just ask anybody. You better now?"

"Well—not really. I'm not happy about getting stuck on a yacht with a bunch of strangers who have eyes that look like they were special ordered from the devil. And did I mention there are some hungry lions and tigers and a gang of six-hundred-pound bears running around upstairs?" She closed her eyes for a minute, overwhelmed by the recitation of her plight. From across the elegant salon, she noticed Scotty scrutinize her, his expression one of pity and resignation.

"Chicky, you haven't seen anything yet," Scotty said. His sister threw him an impatient look.

"Hon, listen to me. I'm going to explain everything." Abby started to sound reasonable.

"The eyes?"

"Yes, the eyes and much more." Abby sighed deeply, extending an encouraging smile. "The bad news is you won't believe a word of it so, to cut to the chase, I'm going to have to show you something. Do I have your permission?"

"Well, chicky, of course you do. Let 'er rip." Kenya felt measurable relief. Her body started to relax, her adrenaline tamped itself back down. *Gee, why does Abby have to make such a big deal about it?* She was sure there was a simple explanation for those eyes. *Didn't* Petah *say they came from an infection?* She peeked around Abby's legs to see what his highness was doing, when Abby's shirt suddenly hit the floor. *What the heck?*

"Hey, ladybug, I'm up here." Kenya looked up from the floor to see a sight so shockingly incomprehensible, her only split-second thought revolved around the random luck that she happened to already be sitting on the floor as she felt her mind surrender to the more welcoming blackness waiting to claim her as she slumped over, dead to all.

Chapter 18

Scotty and Kenya collapsed on the green Haitian cotton lounger in the salon while Abby busied herself making drinks in the kitchen. They expected to be docking in Tampa in less than an hour. Everyone decided they could use a good stiff one before they started the next leg of their journey, psyching themselves up for the rush to the airport . . .

They left Jose in one of the cabins with Chloe. She had miraculously regained consciousness shortly after Kenya fainted. Kane, trying to be helpful, took responsibility for Kenya, helping her to her feet and moving her to an upholstered chaise while everyone else hovered over Chloe. Peter moved topside with the captain, who was alone with the animals as he steered the boat as quickly as possible to Tampa, trying to artfully dodge other pleasure boats as they wandered close enough to spot the unusual nature of the *Lucky Lady's* passengers.

Ginger Mae and Daisy sat silent, huddled together and obsessively following everyone's movements with their shell-shocked eyes. Scotty craned his neck up over Kenya, surreptitiously observing Ginger Mae. The poor woman could barely talk, her lip bloated and swollen. She nodded her head to indicate her gratitude to Abby as she set a crystal snifter of brandy on the Lucite table next to her.

Overhead, occasional sounds filtered into the salon through the open stairwell, proof that the animals hadn't deserted the yacht. The elderly monkeys continued their vigil on the sideboard, looking quite relaxed and content with their newly claimed territory. The macaw busily decorated the sides of the refrigerator with evidence of a prolific digestive system.

Scotty wondered what shape the yacht would be in by the time they got to Tampa. Listlessly he realized the yacht might not even be here for the long haul. Abby's shocking rant about the upcoming cataclysmic event had shaken them to the core. He remembered the incredulous faces in the salon as she had laid out her plan. Even Kenya, recovering on the chaise, had been speechless. He could bet *that* wasn't a common occurrence.

"I don't think that one over there likes me." Kenya pointed to the posse.

"What, you mean Echo?" She was mounted around Barney's neck as usual. Barney was facing the hallway to the cabins. Kenya was positioned directly across the room facing the back of Barney's head. It should have been the back of Echo's head too but, in typical Echo fashion, she had swiveled her head around, doing a one-eighty, to stare at Kenya as her body faced the hallway with Barney's.

Yeah, Scotty thought . . . *creepy*. "Nah, she likes you. She's just been unusually quiet lately."

"So, she does talk?"

"Yeah, but I think she can only talk to people that she's cured. Something about the cure starts the changes. We don't understand any of it. I'm not sure if she does either. She can be very cryptic when she communicates. We get colored pictures of words, sometimes thoughts. Maybe some of it is lost in translation. She's actually very lovable. She's part of the family. As you can see, she adores my dog. Actually, she thinks Barney belongs to her."

They watched Barney inch down to lie flat on the floor. Echo bent over without taking her eyes off Kenya. Her long supple fingers reached out to the floor, tapping on the hardwood like a blind man with a cane until they rested on little Mimi. Her fingers gently stroked Mimi's silken head. Mimi rose instantly, scooting closer to Barney where Echo promptly scooped her up, depositing her lovingly on Barney's head where she could cuddle her.

"Wow, she's just like a little person. I don't know, chicky. How do you know she won't eat them?"

Scotty could see the suspicious calculations going on in her pretty head. He was having a tough time getting a handle on her. He didn't know many black girls, or girls in general. He figured she was possibly the hottest girl he'd ever seen up close. Very opinionated, very pregnant. And she was funny, although he suspected she would not be pleased with his assessment. Except for the hot part.

"Echo doesn't eat anything. She takes what she needs from the sun. Her mouth seems to be for respiration, cooling her body. Like a dog. Although she doesn't have a tongue. No teeth either. Hmm, I wonder if that connection means anything."

"Listen, chicky." She turned to face him, her big exotic cow eyes speaking their own language. "I have a problem here. You all know each other. I'm the new girl. Now I know you have something going with little Chloe." He winced, hearing how that sounded. "I could sure use a friend. A cute guy like you," her eyes were making a move," can handle that, can't you?" She brightened, "We'll be buds. Yeah, I like that. What do you say?" He couldn't ignore the animal magnetism trying to drown him.

"Yeah, sure. Whatever." God, he sounded like a boob. He could feel a creeping red flush set his face on fire.

"I think your wings are, like, major cool. I wouldn't mind having a set a them myself."

"Yes, you would. So far, they're just in the way." He pulled back quickly as he heard Kane's big feet clump down the stairs.

"Hey, guys." Scotty could see Kane's eyes register the cozy scene between him and Kenya. Flopping down on the lounger next to Kenya's vacant side, Kane fumbled in the ripped pocket of his faded shorts to pull out a handkerchief. Giving his sun-bronzed face a good swab, he mopped up the sweat from his handsome mug. Scotty wondered if the sweat was from the roasting sun or the cats which stared like lasers, cataloguing their every move. Kane furtively glanced at Kenya to see if she was paying attention.

"I don't see why we had to do this the hard way. We could have zipped up the interstate right to the airport."

"We never would have made it that far. You can bet the cops are looking for us by now. On the highways, of course. Where else would the trucks go? Who would ever expect someone to load up a pleasure cruiser with uncaged lions and tigers? That good enough for you, Kane?" They all jerked toward the galley as Abby's sarcasm plowed into Kane.

"Look guys, you don't have to second guess me. Echo and I've considered every angle. We'll make it to safety in one piece. If you have any questions, it's all right, just ask me." She walked toward Kane with a gin and tonic in her hand. Passing it over, she admonished him.

"One only. We'll be docking soon." She smiled, her hand drifting to his shoulder in reassurance. "I know it's been a shock. It's hard on all of us. And it'll get harder. But we'll be *safe.*"

Abby stopped speaking as Jose joined them from the hallway, a pitiful portrait of a man trying to function on a depleted emotional reservoir. Scotty could see that he was on the verge of a breakdown, too many shocks to the system. How would anyone feel, arriving home after a long absence to find your girlfriend pulling the rug out from under the new life you'd just finished creating? Pile on the mother of all coincidences: the inconceivable events at Chloe's house which had led to the shocking discovery of her true identity. Way too much to deal with. He knew that Jose would need to quickly come to terms with Abby's bizarre rescue and the ambiguity of a mysterious impending disaster. She needed his support. On top of it all, her easy familiarity around Captain Cobby had not escaped his notice.

"Let me get you something to drink. How about something for Chloe?" Abby snapped to attention as Jose eased himself into a comfortable chair near Ginger Mae. Leaning toward her, he extended a tired hand.

"How're you making out? I'm Jose Diaz."

Ginger Mae stared at the hand left hanging in mid-air as if it was a stinky fish. She appeared puzzled as to what she should do with it. Abby hurried over with ice water for Jose.

"That's okay, Ginger Mae." She patted her shoulder, trying to smooth over the moment. Ginger Mae recoiled as if struck by a venomous serpent. Scotty could see pricks of suspicion in the poor woman's eyes. No one spoke as Ginger Mae tossed her head, attempting a pose of dignity. She self-consciously brushed at her skirt, modestly smoothing it over her knees. Wrapping her arms around little Daisy, her eyes slammed shut like a closed door announcing no one was home.

Kane and Kenya exchanged glances, rolling their eyes questioningly. Jose let his hand drop limply to his side, clearly too burdened with his own pain to recognize the same damage in Ginger Mae.

"Let me see if I can help," Kenya whispered to Scotty. Rising from the chaise longue, she joined them on the sofa, her long model's legs tucked tightly against the upholstery. Ginger Mae watched her move across the room, her face impassive. Kenya sat casually, glancing at Ginger Mae with a gentle warm smile. No big movements. Scotty could see Ginger Mae visibly relax. A few moments passed. Ginger Mae studied Kenya from the corner of her eyes. Then she unexpectedly reached out to touch Kenya's riotous mane of extravagant hair. She caressed it tentatively, a shadow of a smile on her ruined lips.

"That's alright, chicky." Kenya was so overcome by the tenderness of the gesture, she gently swept the woman into her arms where Ginger Mae finally broke down, drenching Kenya with her hot bitter tears. *Well look at that*, Scotty thought. *Good for Kenya. Now maybe some small healing can begin.*

The touchingly raw moment was interrupted by Captain Cobby's arrival. He stomped heavily down the stairs from his station at the helm, leaving Peter to keep watch, tension deeply imbedded in his posture. *Not much different from anyone else,* Scotty observed wryly.

"Abby, I need to speak with you. I just heard from the harbor master." He removed his cap, sweeping his short gray-flecked dark curly hair, damp from the sweat on his forehead, back out of the way. He had an unmistakable aura of adult confidence. *Or is it something else?* Scotty wondered. He noticed Kenya had fluffed up her hair and artfully arranged her legs as she propped up Ginger Mae, stealing looks at the captain.

"How about a glass of water?"

"Sure, Cobby." Abby presented him with his water, her shoulders looking droopy. The captain took the frosted glass from her hands, setting it on a table. Turning her around, he began to massage her neck and shoulders.

"How's that feel?"

"Like heaven." She sighed, letting her head drop, obviously enjoying the sensation. She failed to notice Jose taking in the small intimacy. Scotty could read his face like a book. *What the heck's going on?* No one else reacted to the scene playing out by the steps. *Oh shit!*

"*Abby. Captain Cobby.*" His voice cracked like a bullet. "*Do not move a muscle.*" Now, everyone had noticed the danger. The two at the stairs froze as an eight-hundred-pound Bengal tiger descended the steps, his movements so stealthy not even a dust mote moved.

"Everyone stay calm. He won't do anything. He can't. Trust me, please." Abby's trembling voice clearly belied the confidence she had in the implants.

The enormous cat reached the bottom of the stairs. His head was gigantic, completely blocking access to the stairs. Scotty's heart ratcheted dangerously. He tried to remember to breathe as he subconsciously admired the awesome beauty of the beast. The killing machine.

The cat purposefully scanned the room, every muscle frozen as it maintained its terrifying crouch. Seconds turned into minutes which felt like hours. The hot sweet smell of its pelt suffused the room. Kenya suddenly jumped up onto the sofa, her back to the wall.

"Someone better get that stinkin' cat out a here." Her voice cracked with barely suppressed hysteria. Little Daisy suddenly found her voice, screaming at the top of her lungs. The cat ignored them both. Scotty slowly felt the room careen dangerously. His vision faded and then cleared. Shaking himself, aware that something was wrong, he finally noticed the cat focusing on him. His heart came to a stop as the beast stalked its way across the room, stopping inches away from Scotty's blood-drained face.

The tiger's eyes hypnotized him, obscuring everything else in the room. Distantly, he heard the sound of a dog barking. His attention was focused so tightly on the tiger, he could see his own glowing eyes reflected in its pupils. The hot breath bathing his face, redolent of the beast's last meal, made him queasy. The tiger abruptly sat down on his haunches, not taking his attention off Scotty. A flicker of something in the menacing beast's eye drew his attention. The tiger raised one paw off the wood floor and held it poised in front of Scotty's vulnerable face. Precious seconds ticked by as everyone held their breath, frozen in place. Slowly, eight hundred pounds of coiled muscle placed its paw on Scotty's chest. Its eyes flickered again, the strangeness more apparent, but just as ambiguous. A flash of recognition hit Scotty like a brick as he recognized the half-moon tear in the tiger's ear. It was the same tiger that had mesmerized him at the sanctuary. The tiger stood, lifted its hind leg and urinated, liberally flooding Scotty's foot, a show of dominance and ownership.

It turned to stare at the dogs, quickly padding to the corner where they huddled together. The dogs cowered, dribbling urine and whining softly. Mimi lay flat on her back, legs splayed out exposing her tender belly in submission. Penny sniffed in disdain, refusing to cower. A movement caught everyone's eye as Echo emerged from under the chair that Barney had crawled under. They held their breath, praying for the best. The tiger eyed Echo, sounding an unexpected chuff. After a split second, it turned away and bounded up the stairs.

The terrified group waited a beat before erupting.

"Oh my God. Did he hurt you?"

"Chicky—"

"What's happening, Echo?"

"I need a drink."

"Mommy, Mommy, Mommy, Mommy."

Scotty sat flummoxed. What had just happened? This was not a coincidence. He watched, emotionally bankrupt, as Ginger Mae cooed unintelligible sounds to Daisy, clinging to her niece like a bear unwilling to relinquish the farmer's bee hive. Didn't he just hear Daisy call her Mommy*? Something odd there. I thought Daisy was her niece.*

"What do you think this means?" Abby looked up to Captain Cobby as if he knew all the answers. A bond of some kind definitely radiated between the two. He searched for Jose in the hot room, catching him with his eyes on Abby, reflecting injury clear as a bell. Jose dragged himself over to Scotty, mumbling something about getting back to Chloe then disappeared back down the hallway.

Scotty spotted Echo in a huddle with the posse. He sat down on the floor with them while everyone tried to calm down.

"Did you talk to that tiger, girl?"

Echo's eyes spun brightly with fragmented colors. "Yes, Brother Scotty."

"Well, what did you talk about?"

"He asked me a question."

"Well, what was the question?" Talking to Echo could drive you crazy sometimes.

"He wanted to know if I concurred."

"Concurred with what, Echo?" Scotty sighed with exasperation.

"That you are *The One*."

"Me? The one, what?"

"I can't explain it, Brother Scotty. I just know."

"Know what?"

"That you are *The One*."

Oh, my God. I don't have the strength. Taking a deep breath, he tried again.

"Can you tell me anything about the tiger?"

"His name is Caesar."

"Caesar?" Scotty looked confused.

"Yes, Brother. Are your ears not working?"

"Don't be a comedian, smarty." Scotty reached out and tweaked Echo's belly, making her fall flat on her rump, withdrawing the rainbows from his mind. Barney hurried over to drench her with his sloppy affection. Looking up, he saw Abby watching them. She looked worried.

"What the heck is going on with that tiger? Echo tell you anything?" She waved to Cobby who needed to return to the wheel and check the electronics. She flopped down on the floor with Scotty.

"What the heck was that scene with you and Cobby?" He could hear the anger in his voice. She shrugged with exasperation.

"What are you talking about? Don't be an idiot." She dismissed the question, her expression giving nothing away.

"Okay, Ab, play it your way." He moodily picked at his smelly wet sneakers. Didn't matter much. They were all a little smelly by now.

"So give. What did Echo say?" He pushed his feet away, his long legs stretched in front of him.

"She said Caesar wanted to know if I was the one."

"Caesar? You're on a first name basis now?"

"Echo told me his name." Abby looked skeptical but pressed him for more.

"So what do you mean, 'the one'?"

"I don't know what it means. Echo confused me. You know how she can be. I don't mean to change the subject, but do you know

163

what you're doing here?" He glanced up, nodding his head toward the rest of the dispirited refugees in the room. "I don't think they can take much more."

Abby scanned the room, assessing their condition. "Can't be helped." She suddenly dropped her head into her hands, lifting them to each side of her temples, squeezing tightly. She raised her head as if nothing had happened. "It could get worse, kiddo. I need you to be strong. I think Jose needs some time before I can count on him."

"Are you kidding me? *These people cannot take any more.* What is wrong with you?"

Her expressionless eyes dismissed him. "Kane, maybe you could check on Jose and Chloe for me. I'd like to give him more time for his reunion, but we need him out here, now."

Giving Scotty her signature stink eye, she trudged up the stairs to cautiously check on the wildlife.

"I'll go get Jose and Chloe. You stay and relax." He wanted to allow Kane some time with Kenya. Let her cast her net on him for a while. He'll enjoy it. He tried not to stare as he crossed to the hallway in front of Ginger Mae and Daisy. Something bad had happened there. Maybe Abby knew the story. He'd have to remember to corner her again. *Peter isn't behaving much like a boyfriend, if you ask me.* Outrageously missing in action.

Disappearing into the hallway, he tried to slick back his bright hair with his hands. His clothes, still caked with the dust and battle scars from the rescue, could probably stand up on their own. *And how attractive could a tiger-urine smelling boyfriend be?*

He paused in front of the fiberglass door to the cabin which housed a fragile Jose and a devastated Chloe. Feeling inept and out of his league, he could see how easily his budding romance might get scratched right out of the gate if Chloe sank into a depression or blossomed with an identity crisis. Who could blame her? She was a young girl, still grieving for her mother. How would she handle the ramifications of seeing the man she knew as her father die at the hands of her uncle, who was then murdered by an alien from outer space? And he'd forgotten to factor in her kidnapping and the betrayal. *You just can't write this stuff.*

His heart ached for her but he questioned the validity of his ability to help her. Trying to juggle his own catastrophic body changes, sudden wealth and the constant struggle to cloak his mind-bending secret, was enough to wear anyone down. Romancing a first girlfriend was hard enough in the routine of a normal life. He laughed cynically at the notion that he controlled any part of his own life.

He knocked softly at the door. Jose's sober face met his as the door squeaked open.

"How are you guys making out?" Haltingly, he slipped into the room. "Take a break, Bro, I need to see her for a while." Jose just nodded, his red-rimmed eyes indicating he clearly still felt overwhelmed. His hand reached out, tightly grasping at Scotty's arm as if to speak silently of the need for kid gloves.

"I know, Bro, I know. I'll be careful with her. Abby asked me to let you know we'll be nearing the harbor soon. I'm going to try to coax her out with me, so I'll see you topside." He carefully closed the door, pausing briefly to rest his head against the wall, collecting his composure. Turning, he put on his game face.

"Hi, Chloe." He spoke softly, mindful of disturbing any progress engendered by Jose. She lay prone, face down, Teddy curled like a hairy donut on her back. She looked up at him from the bed, her face blotchy and gray. No sign of happiness to see him. She slowly rolled over to face him, knocking Teddy off her back. Undaunted, the minx scratched at Chloe's blanket until he created an escape route underneath.

Scotty sat on the edge of the bed, just smiling down at her. He didn't feel the need to speak. She looked up, silent, her expression unreadable. A lonely tear slipped forlornly from the tip of an eyelash. Reaching out to stroke her tangled hair, he decided her silence was normal. Chloe had received a shock so great she would doubt everything for quite some time. The answer was to be her friend, reliable and caring, until she healed, ready to come back to him emotionally. It would also give him the time he needed to solve the Caesar mystery and try to help Abby get them through this damnable rush to safety. He continued stroking her hair until he was rewarded with her cold hand sliding into his.

Being teenagers had its advantages. They were resilient. Time ticked on *their* side. Yes, he could be patient. After all, wasn't he *The One?*

THE END

Introduction to
Species Intervention #6609
Book 4

Hive

Synopsis for Hive:

In the rush to Tampa Airport, Abby meets a small group of elephants from the famous Elizabeth Siggins Wildlife Foundation, fleeing the political horrors of Africa. Putting them under her protection and that of the Hive, she meets Tobi, the elderly matriarch of the small herd who sacrifices herself to save a human and, in return, is rewarded with the ultimate gift from the Womb.

As the bedraggled group race to the Hive for protection, saving a few desperate souls as they go, the first bomb arrives. As the survivors and the wildlife struggle to adjust to the new pecking order in the Hive and the revelations of their own origins, a woman and her two grandchildren live through the hellish horror and complete breakdown of civilization aboveground as they struggle to reach the Hive where her husband awaits.

Horror visits the struggling survivors as they learn the Earth will not support habitation for at least another hundred years. But the biggest shock comes from the Womb as it extracts a huge penalty from the hapless people, tolling the demise of the human race.

Chapter 1
2057 AD

Abby and Captain Cobby stood shoulder to shoulder at the helm of the luxury yacht as it swayed with the waves, staring down the approach into Tampa Bay. Abby's heart thudded, the timbre of its pace increasing as she scanned the bay, noting the positions of other nearby craft. She knew, sooner or later, another boat would spot the unusual nature of the occupants spread around the deck of the *Lucky Lady*. She hoped to avoid that as long as possible.

"Cob, I'm getting scared. How in the world are we going to pull this off?" She began to tremble as Cobby gripped her shoulders, turning her to face him. He removed her sunglasses, braving the mesmerizing effects of her shining golden eyes to look deeper into her soul. His deeply tanned, overtly handsome masculinity blended well with all of Abby's golden fragile beauty, the contrast of their ages belying any assumption they might be lovers.

"My dear, you've gotten us this far. You can't fall apart now. Too many rely on you. We have a child and a pregnant woman onboard. They need protection and confidence from you. They can't see you waver. The rest of us know we can depend on you. I might not understand why we must do this, but I have no doubts whatsoever that this is the right thing to do. I know it's our only hope." He pulled her close, his lips brushing the golden hairs at the bridge of her noble forehead. "I'm here for you, we'll get through this. As soon as you give me the word, I'll cross the bay to the industrial docks. The trucks are all in order?"

"Yeah, they're just waiting for us." She removed her sunglasses from Cobby's hands, sliding them back into place as they heard the clatter of water buckets from the deck below.

Leaning out from under their protection from the sun, they observed poor Peter attempting to distribute water to the wildlife. Sweat dripped copiously down his red face and neck, saturating his once fresh Oxford shirt. His glasses sat askew on his red nose as his body shook from fright, warring with his implant's directions and his own fight or flight response to the threat perceived from the wild beasts.

"He sure looks pathetic. How's he holding up?" Cobby turned to Abby assessing the strain in her hands as they beat slowly against her thighs. Personally, he thought Peter hovered on the very edge of madness. The fact that his lady love had turned out to be a calculating prostitute attached to a psychotic murderer had already pushed him to the precipice of sanity. And Cobby thought the guy might be strung a bit too tight to begin with. The implant Abby had used to keep him calm and do her bidding might just be enough to push him off the ledge to insanity.

"I'm not really sure about him." Abby's voice faltered. "I need him to hold up. I trust him. If something goes wrong before we get back home, I can rely on him. If I remove the implant now, I know he'll freak. I think Ginger Mae might be the first girl he's ever had sex with. Once we're safe and I remove the implant, he'll still have to deal with her betrayal." Turning to Cobby, she placed a hand on his chest, her face tilted admiringly to the captain. "You're the one I thank God for."

Cobby's large callused hand enveloped her own. "Abby, I—oh, hi." He calmly dropped his hand from Abby's as Jose's head, then his body appeared on the stairs from the deck below. His thick tawny tail flicked in a sultry fashion as if to deliberately draw attention, apparently indifferent to the sensibilities of those in the salon still reeling from the shock over the big disclosure Abby had made regarding Echo and the changes to their bodies.

"Captain, do you mind? I'd like some privacy please."

Cobby felt the soft pressure of Abby's restraining hand on his arm. Backing up slowly, he returned to the helm, making himself comfortable in the captain's chair. If there was going to be fireworks, he didn't want to be in the line of fire. He enjoyed Jose's company, but was well aware of the sidelong glances he had been sending toward Abby and him since he returned from his trip. Given half a chance, he thought Abby might consider him as a lover, but for now they needed to be fully engaged in their tasks at hand. Another emotionally fragile jilted young man in their entourage could spell catastrophe. He didn't yet know the complete story of Scotty and his traumatized girlfriend, Chloe. Maybe Kane could clue him in. The kids all seemed to be thick as thieves. *Guess that beats their readiness to rip out each other's throats a month ago.*

"Abby, do you mind telling me what the fuck is going on? I think I've been patient enough, and now you have me scared shitless. And who are those people downstairs? And why is that poor disfigured women with the screaming child with Peter? When did he find time to get a girlfriend?" Cobby could sense Jose working up to an explosion, but he refused to be drawn in. It was Abby's baby now.

He watched as Abby made shushing sounds at Jose, wrapping her arms around him and murmuring in his ear.

"Babe, you have to trust me. There's just no time. I'm doing this because Netty and Echo have asked me too."

"Netty? Who's Netty? Does this involve Echo's mission?"

"Yeah, it does have something to do with his mission. And with saving our lives. We must bring these animals, and the ones from the zoo, to Echo's hive. They claim we'll be safe there. But they insist these animals be saved. You'll meet Netty soon enough."

"What zoo? What zoo are you talking about?"

"There's a large zoo not far from Newark Airport. I have trucks meeting us there. I'll send everyone on to Sussex County, except Scotty and Echo. They need to help me. If you could direct everyone else to the place you met Echo, you can wait for me there."

"But what about all of these animals? How the hell am I going to make them go with me into the woods?" Jose's tone of voice gave away the skepticism he felt toward Abby's plan. "Wait just a gosh darn minute. Are you talking about the Bronx Zoo? Is *that* the zoo?"

"Yes, that's the zoo."

"Are you out of your ever-loving mind? Do you know how many animals are there?"

"Please, Jose. Everything is all set to go. Just take everyone to the Hive," Abby beseeched him, glancing at her watch. "I need you to let everyone know we're headed into the bay and will be docking within an hour. That about right, Cobby?"

"Yes. We need to be ready to roll. The cops will be called as soon as the harbor master is informed by a snoop about our cargo. I think we have a window of about forty five minutes before we get hassled. If the trucks have their doors open and the ramps in place, we can get the cats and the bears loaded before trouble starts. The rest should be a cinch."

"*Okay.*" Abby's bright voice suggested the subject was closed. She leaned out over the bridge and hollered down to Peter, waving him to join them. Turning back to Jose, she begged him again. "Can you please just do this for me? We have our whole lives to sort this out. First, we just need to survive." Her voice softened. Wordlessly, Jose turned to the stairs, ignoring Peter as he stepped aside to let him pass.

"Abby, you wanted to see me?" Cobby eyed the man confronting Abby. His round moon face dripped with sweat. His clothes appeared to have been slept in for the last week, yet Cobby knew Peter to be a fastidious dresser. His eyes stared at Abby, unblinking, his face slack-jawed. Cobby's head snapped back as he got a whiff of the odor rolling off Peter: acrid, sweet, organic and foul. It couldn't all be the result of his exposure to the animals. Was it the smell of fear? He glanced at Abby for her reaction, but she apparently didn't notice. Her hand rested on Peter's arm.

"Are you alright, Peter?"

"No, Abby, I'm not alright. My girlfriend is a professional whore.
I abetted the murder of a psycho who held a gun on me for two days.
I just finished watering some cats that weigh three times what I do,
and they know it. A camel spit in my face, then shat on my feet. My
boss, who I cared for, just turned out to be some kind of alien freak,
and we seem to be running for our lives with a boatful of hungry,
dangerous, smelly creatures. And it's hot." He spoke calmly and
precisely, his face expressionless, belying the drama of his words.

"You think I'm an alien freak?"

"I don't know what you are." He stared at Abby, his eyes
unblinking and unwavering, his face subjugated and beaten. As Abby
gently took him into her arms, Cobby watched carefully. He knew a
close eye on this character would be a necessity. He appeared ready
to go postal, and as captain, he needed to get this vessel to shore.
Maybe Abby would let him dump Peter in the rush to load the
animals. He planned to vote long and hard on leaving this guy
behind.

"Abby, I'm ready to cross the bay. Why don't you take Peter
below and make sure everyone is packed up and ready to disembark?
Push those monkeys and the birds up on deck."

"Aye, aye, Captain. Come on, Peter, why don't we go down
together? I still need your help with Ginger Mae and Daisy."

As she guided Peter back to the stairs, she turned to meet Cobby's
steely gaze and his imperceptible nod in Peter's direction. She
slipped him a quick thumb's up, then disappeared down the stairs.

Chapter 2

Scotty sat with Chloe in the once elegant salon of the family yacht, the air conditioning failing to suppress the cacophony of animal odors mixing with the smells of human sweat.

They sat watching Kenya try to convince Kane and Ginger Mae to bolt from the yacht as soon as it hit the dock in Tampa. She paced madly, one hand on her big belly and the other gesticulating wildly as she tried to sell the idea to an indifferent Kane and a numb Ginger Mae, her swollen face and grotesquely stitched lip refusing to allow her a moment's peace.

Chloe sat unmoving and silent, unless Scotty happened to shift his weight. She then clutched at him convulsively, refusing to relinquish her anchor to sanity.

As Kenya continued to rant, she failed to notice Abby and Peter as they descended into the salon from above. Peter selected an upholstered chair nearest the stairs, collapsing like a deflated blow-up doll, smelly and wrinkled with a wicked sunburn. Abby quietly stood behind Kenya as she railed at Kane, reaching hysterical proportions, refusing to concede a losing battle.

Abby's hand suddenly shot out, grabbing Kenya by the arm, swinging her around and slapping her across the face.

"I want you to go sit down and, for Pete's sake, shut up. This is not good for the baby."

"How dare you? You're not my mother!" Kenya held her hand up to her reddened cheek as she nonetheless took a seat. "You can bet I'm gonna report you when we get back to town, chicky, you wait and see."

Abby stood in front of Kenya and whipped off her sunglasses, exposing her flashing golden eyes, anger and impatience surging at high tide.

"Don't you get it, young lady? We're not going back to town. How much clearer can I be? You can stay here and die with everyone else or you can come with us and live. Your baby will live. But you must stop. No one wants to hear it. And I don't need any more problems. I have enough to worry about as it is. Got it? Now what will it be?"

Kenya appeared genuinely frightened, but everyone knew Abby meant business. Scotty watched as Kenya scanned the room for support, finding no one to meet her eyes. With a sob, she nodded her head at Abby and leaned back against her seat, finally acquiescing.

"Peter, I need you and Scotty to keep everyone together. *Peter*, are you listening to me?" Peter sat with his chin on his chest, his eyes shut. They flew open as Abby made her way toward him.

"I hear you. Consider it done. Animals first, then we make a dash for the limos."

"Yes, okay. Scotty, you two good?"

"Yeah, Sis, we're okay. We'll be ready."

"Good boy. Be prepared to make a wild dash. Just make sure all the animals make it off the boat first." She turned back to Kenya and leaned down to gently brush her wild tresses back from her face. "It'll be okay, hon, this is the worst part. Once we head for the airport we're gold." Glancing at Jose who stood with the monkeys in the galley, she gave a brave smile. "I'll be up top if you need me."

Scotty watched his sister mount the stairs and disappear. He could feel the boat pick up speed. It wouldn't be long before they had to run for it. He wanted to make an effort to stay out of the way of the tigers. He didn't want any repeat of the previous confrontation with Caesar.

"Hey, Scotty." Kane rose to squat in front of Scotty and Chloe. "You ready for this?"

"Yeah, just do what you can for Kenya, I'll take Chloe. Jose and Peter will handle Ginger Mae and Daisy."

Scotty felt a tug on his shirt from under the sofa. He glanced down to see the posse creep out from underneath, urged on by Echo, her long slender leather-like fingers patting Mimi as she happily joined the rest of the dogs, which sat like sentinels clustered around Echo, Barney at the helm. An aura assailed Scotty, spastic with agitation.

"It is time, Brother Scotty. I will stay with My Barney."

"No, Echo, I think you need to let me carry you. I can't run the risk that you'll get knocked around if you're underfoot or with Barney."

"No, Brother, I need to be with My Barney no matter what. I need."

"*You need*? Don't be silly, Echo." Scotty reached down to lift the furry creature to his lap. Chloe reached over to softly stroke her head.

"You need to stick close to me, girl, Abby might need us."

"No, no, no. I cannot. I must be with My Barney." Echo wiggled out of Scotty's grasp, then slid down his lap to quickly wobble over to Barney. The two stood cuddled up to one another, and Scotty cocked his eyebrow at Echo.

"Something you want to tell me, Echo?"

"No, my Brother. I should not bother you. We will stick close, do not worry."

Dismissing Echo's odd behavior, Scotty readied himself for the next leg of their escape.

The *Lucky Lady* picked up speed as she made her way across the sun-glared water of Tampa Bay, throwing out huge waves of wake from both sides of the craft. Captain Cobby's eyes searched for the buoys marked on his map which would steer him into the private dock of a long abandoned industrial park where an old buddy from his young yacht jock days worked as a security guard. A green flag would mark the dock slated for their use. He should be able to spot Abby's caravan of trucks, lined up and ready to accept their unusual cargo.

"Hey, Dad, I see we're almost there. I'm going down to put the gangplank in place. Scotty will pass it out to me after we dock. I'm not looking forward to this part. I keep waiting for one of the cats to jump one of us." Kane nervously paced around his father.

"Don't worry, Kane, as long as we stay calm we'll be safe. I believe in Abby and this is our only chance to save ourselves. I'm not going to blow this chance for you, Son." Cobby wrapped his arms around his handsome boy, grateful for the intimate moment. With a swat on the butt, he sent Kane down to the deck to get in position.

They were a few minutes from docking, Cobby having spotted the green flag. He could see the trucks lined up on the other side of a chain-link fence about two hundred feet from the dock. *Damn*—he had counted on them parking closer. The idea of crossing two hundred feet of wide-open space with a bunch of apex predators in unfamiliar territory made his stomach churn. Steadying his hand on the wheel, he throttled back to ease the big boat slowly into the dock with a soft grumble from the twin diesel engines. Kane dropped down to the dock to secure the ropes, tying them tautly.

From below, Scotty appeared, shoving the heavy gangplank out for Kane to position for the animals.

Cobby could hear the restlessness in his four-legged charges as they became aware of the docking and reacted to instructions from their implants.

"Yo . . . you there. I'm looking for Abby. Oh boy, here we go again." One of the truckers approached at the same time that the bears decided they would be the first to depart. Six hundred pounds of muscular fur and clacking claws would make anyone shit their pants when they were close enough to feel the hot breath of a chuffing ursine on their colorless lips. Rooted to the spot, the trucker let the bear pass before he hightailed it back to the safety of his truck. The truckers knew what to do. Sit tight, say nothing, do nothing. Abby would tell them when to close the backs of the trucks. They knew the drill. Then they would follow the limos to the airport, about a twenty-minute ride in normal traffic.

Cobby wiped his sweaty brow with a well-used rag, observing his wilted and odorous human passengers huddled on the starboard side of the boat, dogs and luggage milling at their reluctant feet, the relentless heat adding to their discomfort. Christ, it sure was hotter than a naked babe on the back of a motorcycle.

Cobby stood up, waving to the small crowd down on the deck below.

"Kane, check the boat, top to bottom. Make sure all the animals are off. Where are Abby and Scotty?"

"They're bringing up the turtles."

Cobby watched as Abby emerged with her brother, a huge tortoise held between them.

"We've got it, Cobby. Two more to go." Abby tilted her chin in his direction. "You might as well abandon ship. Go with Jose and the rest to the limos. Get the women settled. Peter and the boys will help me with the other turtles. Meet you at the limo."

One look at Peter, and Cobby could understand why Abby wanted him with her. He stood uselessly apart from the knot of women, a walking zombie. Maybe he would respond more effectively if he hadn't been forced to help Ginger Mae and little Daisy. Sliding off the captain's chair, he shut down the engines, slapped his hand on his chair and said a final goodbye to the beautiful craft he had controlled for over ten years. She didn't deserve the piles of animal crap and pools of urine left to decorate her proud decks, but they planned to leave her at the dock to whatever her fate may be, knowing she may have helped save their lives.

Quickly descending the stairs to the deck, he swept Chloe and Teddy, Ginger Mae, Daisy, Kenya, and Echo and her dog pack down the gangplank to the waiting limos with most of the luggage. So far, the animals and people had found the dash to the chain-link fence uneventful. Casting his gaze around, Cobby glimpsed Scotty and

Kane delivering the last tortoise to a truck.

"Okay, Dad. That's it. Let's get out of here." Kane ran past his father, slapping him on the back as he slipped into one of the limos with Kenya, Scotty, Chloe, and Echo and the dogs. The other limo would carry the rest of them. Not a happy bunch. Cobby shrugged, feeling the weight of responsibility as the oldest of the group, stretching his strong arms as he made his way out of the hot sun into the air-conditioned limo.

Abby ran to catch up as the trucks revved their motors and eased the convoy away from the last forlorn glimpse of Tampa Bay that any of them would ever see.

Abby sat between Jose and Captain Cobby, her hand resting on Jose's lean leg. Occasionally her hand would spasm, her exhaustion and adrenaline warring with themselves to control her body, the implant placed by Netty guiding her mind. She tried to relax her body as her curiosity focused on the mystery that was Netty. She felt a clean uncomplicated honesty emanate from the regal woman. An overwhelming sense of gentle confidence which contrasted with the strangeness and urgency of the tasks she had entrusted Abby with. Everything was such an enigma. But Abby knew one thing for sure. One frightening, cataclysmic, irrefutable fact: hundreds of millions now lived their last days, and she fully intended to survive. If she could save a few others in the process—great.

She actually understood that humans as a species didn't deserve this planet, but her heart bled with the thought of the uncorrupted babies and children who would perish. Tears escaped from under her sunglasses as she thought of the creatures that really deserved to live; the exquisite and the mighty, the docile and the fierce. All part of God's garden, all tragic victims. Abby hadn't been raised as a particularly pious devotee of religion, but she, along with most, believed in God. But where were the answers to God's eternal indifference to the pain and brutality inflicted by Homo sapiens on all life since the dawn of early man? Where were *those* answers? Abby's fist contracted painfully on Jose's leg. He glanced at her with a raised eyebrow.

"Babe, you good?"

She picked up his hand, raising it to her lips to reassure him. "I'm fine, just nerves. Maybe we should call Mama Diaz and give her an ETA? Jose, I don't know what you've told her, but could you ask her to pack all the tools we left at the house? And make sure they're ready to move everything to the woods. I'll have extra hands to move the heavy boxes when we get there. I'm going to ask some of the truckers from the second caravan if they want to join us. That's why we tried to hire nonviolent drivers with no family connections. I want them to be able to make a fast decision. And it's why I asked them to bring their pets with them. I thought it would help. I would never get over leaving Barney and the gang behind if the situation were reversed. It should be a big help."

"Oh, yeah, that's a big help." Peter's bitterness intruded from across the seat. As Abby opened her mouth to respond, she thought better of it. Sighing audibly, she closed her mouth, determined to say no more.

The caravan entered the approach to the commercial cargo ramp for air freight. This next phase would include Echo. One by one the vehicles and trucks passed through the gigantic metal security device which read the presence of all explosive and metal objects. Their progress continued as slowly as a snail on vacation, Abby's impatience ready to ignite.

Finally most of the trucks made it through, pulling up to join the limos on the tarmac. *Now, here comes the dicey part.* Abby climbed out of the limo quickly, pulling open the door to the other car.

"Come on guys, hurry, hurry . . . Find a seat onboard. Sorry, but you have to cram in there. It's going to be a little cramped. It's not a luxury airliner, but it'll get us where we need to go. The important thing is the animals." Abby looked over her shoulder as the inspectors approached, looking for her permits.

"Echo, come on girl, you're on!" Echo scrambled out of the limo, Barney sticking to her like glue.

"Scotty, take Barney with the rest of the dogs. Get them secured on the transport."

A violently fluctuating aura assailed her mind, forcing her hand to her head in shock. The whispers screamed. "*No*, Sister. Barney *must* stay with me. I need."

"Okay, okay, whatever. Bring Barney if you must." Turning to Barney, Abby gave a quizzical look at his loyal mug, eyes bright, shining with love and unquestionable trust. Her heart melted at the thought that someone had once thrown this joyful personality away as a pup like a piece of disposable garbage. Shaking her head, she realized what an arbitrary lady Fate could be. Look at Barney's life now: loved so well, and loved far, far beyond anyone's wildest dream by the most enigmatic creature on the planet, part of his adoring family. Abby knelt down to place a kiss on Barney's tender muzzle, happy to have him remind her of the smallest of the fragile lives which would be saved by her efforts.

The airport officials approached. Abby turned to Scotty, whispering directions under cover of the airport noises. Pointing out their transport, she directed him, "Get the trucks to start unloading. I won't be long." Turning to the airport officials, she nudged Echo forward.

"Gentleman, I believe you are looking for me."

"If you are in charge of the contents of this transport, miss, may I have your permits please?" Echo stood with her arm wrapped around Barney's neck as her antlers split, releasing just the correct amount of implant creatures, which flew to the ears of the officials who could destroy all hope of leaving the airport with her precious charges. Naturally, Abby had been unable to obtain all the complex permits and vaccination records needed to transport wildlife of this kind. CITES, the Convention on International Trade in Endangered

Species of Wild Fauna and Flora, required reams of paperwork and certifications to protect the transportation of wildlife. Abby was shooting from the hip here. Echo's facilitation made everything so much easier.

The implants did their work as Abby waited for the signs that the inspectors were under control. Shaking their heads and pulling on their ears then grinning like simpletons, they assured her she could proceed safely.

"I want you both to return to your desks. Everything is in order here, correct?"

"Yes, ma'am. You have a nice flight now. Nice doggies you have there." With a quick pat on Echo's head, they turned smartly on their heels and walked away. One down, now just the pilots to go. Cobby should be briefing them at the moment. She hoped to avoid grief from them regarding the lack of proper cages for the animals. She had selected Pet Air because the cargo bay came equipped with built-in cages that would help secure most of the smaller animals and some of the cats. The rest would be forced to settle down on the moving blankets and make their own nests. Turning, she heard Cobby shout her name, running toward her.

"You were right, I need Echo to handle the pilots. The loading is going smoothly, just very slowly. I'm going to take Echo with me, okay?"

"Yeah, take Barney with you too, please, Cobby. Don't let Echo implant them unless you're forced. And keep Echo hidden until you need her. I'll join you as soon as I can."

Cobby ruffled her long golden hair. "You holding up, kiddo?" His smile reflected nothing but worry and admiration for her.

She smiled back, her lips threatening to collapse on her. *Suck it up girl*, she thought. *This is not the time to cry in Cobby's arms.*

"I'm fine, Cob. I'll see you later." She watched as Cobby marshaled the furry pair off to the animal transport for a sit-down with the pilots. Looking over the receding shoulder of Captain

Cobby, she noticed another transport pulling in toward their parking area. It featured the insignia of the British Royal Air Force on the side of the transport. *Why the heck was the Royal Air Force here?* Mentally slapping herself across the face, she pulled her mind back to what she needed to focus on.

Fifteen minutes later, as Abby watched her animals offload from the trucks and settle into the belly of their transport with much complaining and shuffling of space mates, she found her ears assailed with the strange sounds of trumpeting and rumbles which gripped her deep into the very marrow of her bones. Following the frantic sounds, she found herself led to the very transport that had caught her eye a few minutes ago.

The belly of the transport lay open with activity milling, the focus of some black men dressed in blue-green coats signifying some kind of uniform. Creeping closer, she noticed agitation and helpless sorrow permeated their demeanors. The trumpets sounded more frantic the closer she got. As her presence alerted the attention of the men, she nodded politely, getting a nod from one of the taller men, his world-weary chocolate eyes dripping with disconsolate acceptance.

"Jambo, miss." Abby nodded respectfully, understanding a friendly greeting if not the Swahili language. Peering into the belly of the transport, she got the surprise of her life. In the rear of the plane stood an unhappy group of elephants. Yes, elephants, practically extinct after the horrendous slaughter of the 2015–2019 ivory wars and the subsequent decision to slaughter the largest and wisest for meat to feed the refugees in Sudan, Uganda, Libya and South Africa.

Abby noticed grave differences in the elephants. The largest and oldest, almost elderly; two smaller juveniles; one adult tusker and three tiny babies, one of which lay prostrate on the floor of the plane, a few feet from the men, who she now realized must be their keepers. The tiny baby looked to be only a few weeks old with the tip of its delicate tiny trunk missing. It appeared to have been bitten off and now lay lifeless, swollen and infected. The poor thing's breathing sounded labored, obviously on the doorstep of death.

"Oh no, the poor thing." Tears trickled unnoticed from under her shades. *Who are these people?* She addressed the tall man who appeared to be in charge.

"Hello, I'm Abby Preston." The man gave a quick bow.

"I'm Johno. It is my pleasure to meet you, Miss Abby." His grin reached from ear to ear, but his heart clearly neglected to join in.

"Where did you come from? And what's wrong with the little one?"

"She has pneumonia. She is dying." He hung his head. "There is little we can do now."

"What in the world are you doing here, in Tampa?"

"We are from Nairobi, Africa. The radical Islamic leaders ordered all non-native landowners to turn over their land to the government. They were given forty eight hours to vacate the country. We could not leave these precious few elephants behind. They would have been eaten, just like this poor little one's mother. The babe was found stuck in a shallow well. She must have run in her panic after her mother was slain, falling in. We were notified by a kind Masai. Her trunk was savaged, probably by a hyena. It is common. We set down here from the Miami airport because if she dies, the others will be upset and they need calmness. It is not a good time to be in an airplane for them."

"I don't understand why you have them, elephants are almost extinct. It's against the law to bring an elephant out of Africa."

"Yes, Miss Abby. I work for the Elizabeth Siggins Wildlife Foundation. I have worked for them for over forty years. Ms. Elizabeth's husband started the Kenya Wildlife Protection Corp. so many years ago. Ms. Elizabeth was a very famous woman, loved by many all over the world for her spirit and dedication. She created miracles for her beloved elephants. When the government threatened the land that belonged to the foundation, the family enlisted the help of Her Majesty's Royal Air Force to secrete the elephants away to safety in the United States. They have always been important supporters of Ms. Elizabeth's efforts. Everything happened so quickly. Unfortunately, we were only able to save these few before the soldiers came. We were lucky to get away. Many more were left behind." Johno's voice broke, his arm raked across his eyes, wiping away his tears. "My babies . . . so much trauma and terror in their short lives." He broke down, sobbing uncontrollably. "We could not save them all. I am sorry, I cannot speak further. Please excuse me." He turned back to the pitiful creature sprawled on the floor surrounded by the other keepers, tears in the eyes of the anguished men.

Abby slowly approached the circle of men. She reached out to rest her hand on Johno's shoulder. "Johno, I can help you. I can help the baby."

Johno's head snapped back to her with uncontrolled hope. "You can help our baby, Miss Abby? Please, please. How can you help? Do you have a miracle medicine?"

"No, Johno, I have something better. Please, stand back." She moved Johno to the side, waving away the attentions of the other keepers. Johno's face fell as he realized she would not be forthcoming with medicine.

Seemingly from out of thin air, Abby's tail flexed and snapped high into the air, extruding its healing membrane, sending pressure felt by all and the accompanying odor of sulfur. The keepers didn't understand the significance of her tail or where the path of pressure emanated from, and reacted by throwing themselves flat on the ground, screaming.

As the excited screams slowed to frightened mutters, the men finally absorbed the complete quiet settling around their shoulders, no more sound coming from the belly of the transport, the elephants' silence ominous. Then a squeak. And then a squeal, coming from none other than the dying baby, who struggled to stand under her own power as a cacophony of excited trumpets emanated from the back of the transport, happy elephants eager to caress the newly healthy baby.

The keepers rose slowly, frightened and unbelieving, their hands making the sign of the cross. Abby watched Johno, his face impassive and calm, a cypher. He turned to her, holding out his hand. "Miss Abby, the Lord has sent you to us."

Abby stepped up to grasp his hand in hers. "Where are you traveling with these elephants, my friend?"

"We have been offered sanctuary in the most wondrous place. It is called The Bronx Zoo."

Abby smiled wide. "Yes, I have heard of it. I think we will meet again, my friend. I am going in that direction myself. Will you be leaving soon?"

"Yes, miss, we will leave as soon as possible." Johno's eyes searched hers, his voice giving out and reverence overwhelming his impassive nature. As Abby turned to take her leave she glanced back.

"You may want to have a look at the big elderly girl in there. She is one happy ele." With a nod, she returned to her own transport.

Johno stood rooted to the spot. He thought he had seen everything in his sixty two years. He had never considered himself a superstitious man as so many Africans were wont to be. He prided himself as one of the lucky few with parents who were able to afford a uniform that enabled him to attend school as a youngster. Fate stepped into his young life when he met the first extraordinary woman of his life, Ms. Elizabeth Siggins. She had recognized his deep capacity to love her little orphan charges as the adults fell under the onslaught of ivory poachers, poison arrows, droughts, angry cattle herders and the fences which had appeared across their traditional migratory routes, displacing them. No one could have foreseen the political shift in Kenya from staunch ally of the United States to the radical Islamic stronghold which had turned to the wildlife to feed the hordes of refugees they displaced in other African countries, causing chaos and turmoil to all English landowners, instituting a land grab, evicting them from their land and confiscating all their personal property, including their creatures.

For rescue centers, rehabilitation stations and wildlife biologists with decades-old study groups, the outcome was catastrophic as they struggled to fight the confiscation of their creatures for the slaughterhouses. Many noble men and women lost their lives to the merciless onslaught, refusing to desert the creatures they had long loved. Those that stayed behind with Johno to salvage what they could had heard rumors of the tragedy at The Dian Fossey Research Center at Karisoke in neighboring Rwanda. A habituated family of thirty gorillas had disappeared with no trace, thought to have been vanquished by poachers who had probably slaughtered them for bush meat.

Six months later, the staunchly loyal personnel were murdered as they tried desperately to protect the remaining families of the fragile yet magnificent mountain gorillas who remained in their charge. The reports of copious quantities of blood and stiffening gorilla carcasses displayed high on the back of triumphant Islamic trucks quickly reached the ears of all in the conservation community in Nairobi. Heavy hearts at the Siggins Wildlife Foundation quickly formulated plans to evacuate.

Johno and the other keepers escaped with a very small amount of elephants, two young rhinos, and a pair of kudu through the efforts of the Royal Air Force and the daughters of the long-deceased Ms. Elizabeth. Johno's heart bled at the thought of how his benefactress gratefully resided in heaven with her beloved husband. He knew they were surrounded by all the baby eles who had never recovered from the trauma and shock of their brief introduction to this brutal world. He glanced to the heavens to thank the Lord she did not have to know of this bitter catastrophe.

Johno's thoughts returned to Miss Abby's parting remark about his elderly elephant. She had no way of knowing how he had insisted this special wise creature accompany them to salvation in the United States. He just could not have lived if forced to leave Tobi behind. She remained one of the pride and joys of the Wildlife Foundation, a success story beyond their wildest dreams and a personal favorite of Ms. Elizabeth and Johno. A wild elephant who had never forgotten her love of her keepers, and returned endlessly to check on new babies and preen as the keepers lavished adoration and affection on her.

Poor tiny Tobi had been found near death's doorstep in September of 2002 near a water hole in the Imenti Forest in Meru. Her mother was thought to have been a victim of poaching, their small herd having been cut off from their traditional migration route to the Mount Kenya forests by the fencing that followed the expansion of human settlements.

They had estimated Tobi's age to be only days old. The only measure that had kept the poor newborn alive was the discovery by Ms. Elizabeth that when a newborn did not have the opportunity to draw on its mother first milk, they missed out on the critical colostrum needed to trigger the infant's natural immune system. When a colostrum-deficient infant was discovered, they had to ascertain whether a severe enteritis was present, producing bleeding from the rectum and the onslaught of deadly pneumonia. Ms. Elizabeth had discovered that a transfusion of blood extracted from another newborn could be distilled to plasma and injected through a vein in the ear of the stricken orphan, saving its life. Such had been the case with Tobi. After the successful transfusion, they had given her hope for a new chance at life. In the Meru dialect, Tobi means life.

Johno's decision to bring her in from her life in the wild had given her hope again. She would now escape the ruthless slaughterhouses along with the three young orphans; the two four-year-old juveniles; the young bull, Medoc; and their two young rhino, the youngest completely blind.

Johno heard a trumpet from inside the plane. A trumpet of glee and happiness—but loud, very loud. The big ones must be overjoyed about the recovery of the little nameless one. Hefting himself up onto the cargo deck of the transport he could not believe his eyes. Tobi looked ten years younger. The nasty rip in her right ear was gone, the long gnarly scar near the tip of her delicate trunk, nonexistent. She shifted happily from side to side, lifting her feet as if her swollen arthritic joints no longer pained her. The bull and two juveniles excitedly ran their trunks all over her legs.

My Lord, thought Johno, stunned to the core. *I think I have just met the second most important person in my life.*

Chapter 3

Abby ran from truck to truck ensuring all were empty. To her consternation, she inadvertently attracted the attentions of one of the truckers.

"Come on, babe, slow down. I just want to say a proper how do."

Abby ignored him and continued to check the trucks. She wanted to shove off and get the transport in the air. In the back of her mind she began to worry about the manpower it might take to properly care for all of the animals she planned to save. She wanted to ask members of the Bronx Zoo trucking convoy to voluntarily join them, yet she couldn't be certain that would give her enough manpower.

"Babe, come on. I just want a little time to chat ya up seeins I might be back in these parts again, ya never know. Sure would be nice and neighborly if ya let me look ya up." The unfortunate lothario was none other than the skinny, weasel-faced, cigarette-smoking trucker who had pissed his pants back at the Big Cat Sanctuary when he had unexpectedly confronted a bear and a lion as they calmly padded to his truck. It seemed he had finally recovered his dignity and located his missing balls. She stopped in her tracks to face him.

"Look, *babe.* I don't have time for this. I appreciate the job you did for me, but it's time to move on now." *Or is it?* Abby's head shot straight up with an idea. Turning to the shit-kicker, she plastered on her best smile.

"Whoa—Dezi likes." His face lit up like a kitten that had just discovered the keys to a sardine truck.

"Dezi. May I call you Dez?" Abby flinched to herself at the sound of her cheesy come-on, even though Dezi's had been far worse.

"Babe, you can call me anything you want as long as you call me." He snickered and preened, tugging semi-discreetly at his crotch, the area experiencing an unmistakable swelling. Rolling her eyes, she sensed that the pathetic guy spouted his annoying repartee to make up for his unfortunate mug and unimposing stature, yet she also sensed something broken and hurt in this impudent guy. Freezing the smile on her face, she tried again.

"Dez, if you're available, I would like you to accompany us to Newark to help with the offload of the animals. I'll pay you well. The job will take about twelve hours, including flying time. I need additional help at a zoo and could really use you. I'll fly you back to Tampa first class and cover the cost of leaving your truck here." She bit the bullet and placed her hand seductively on his arm. He jumped a foot in the air with surprise at the unexpected touch.

"I'd be doin' you a solid?" He looked as anxious as a puppy trying hard to hold its urine.

"Yeah, Dez. You'd be doing me a solid."

"So you and me might find some time in the future to do the dirty?"

Abby recoiled. "For Pete's sake, Dez, let's take things a bit slower. We'll talk about that when the job's done. Do we have a deal?"

Dezi narrowed his eyes suspiciously. Abby identified his transparent emotions as they flickered across his homely face, clearly wondering how far he could go with her, hoping she wasn't putting him on. He broke out in a smile.

"Yeah, babe, let's go for it." He held out his hand for a shake. Abby clasped his hand only to be pulled off balance toward him and rewarded with a sloppy attempt at a kiss.

"Damn, Dez, I said, slow. S-l-o-w. Got it?" His shit-eating grin made her wonder about the wisdom of her offer.

"Yeah, babe, I got it." He pursed his lips and made kissing sounds.

Oh, please deliver me, she thought. "Why don't you head to the transport after you park your truck someplace safe? Introduce yourself around and find a seat like a good boy, okay?"

"Okay. See you later, babe." He turned toward his truck with a slap and a caress on his own butt, turning once to wink before disappearing from sight.

Puke. Abby shook her head, her long golden hair swaying as she wondered how in the world she would explain this to Jose.

Coming upon the last truck, she recognized the driver.

"Hello, Mr. Calloway. You must be in a hurry to get on with your next gig." Clyde straightened up respectfully from his lounging position alongside his truck, his portly belly still hanging well below his belt.

"Miss Preston, happy to see you. This sure has been a first for me and my rig. You have a mighty magic touch with the beasts." His clear hazel eyes bore into hers. Abby recognized a man not easily fooled but practical enough not to ask questions. "I'm in no hurry. I'm not running to the next job. My wife and the grandkids are in Tampa for a couple of weeks. I'm going to join them, kick back a beer and let the kids have their way with me." Clyde's lined but still relatively attractive face shined with pure bliss. And of course, that gave Abby an idea.

"Mr. Calloway—"

"Call me Clyde."

"Clyde. And I'm Abby. As I was saying, would you be interested in lending me a hand for another twelve hours? It means going to Newark with us on the transport and help with the logistics of another load of animals at a local zoo. The pay is rich."

"How rich?"

"Rich enough to make it impossible to turn me down."

"Well, now you're talkin'. But just twelve hours. I need to get back to my grandkids."

"No problem, Clyde. Why don't you pull your truck over there and find a seat on the transport? If you could sit with Dezi and keep an eye on him, I would be most grateful."

"Dezi?" His eyebrow rose.

Abby laughed knowingly. "Yeah, I know. But the guy's harmless, he just needs a firm hand."

She waved as Clyde nodded and climbed into his truck with a smile. "Twelve hours, not one minute more."

Jose eyed the passenger seats on the transport. The door separating them from the cargo hold didn't appear strong enough to resist the efforts of Barney, let alone the Bengal tiger Scotty and Echo called Caesar. Abby may have them under control with Echo's implants but she was a novice at this. *Christ, anything can go wrong.* He thumped down in a seat near the middle, wondering when Abby would join them. His list of questions now reached from Tampa back to Sarasota. He steamed quietly as he caught a glimpse of Captain Cobby picking a seat near Kane.

Sizing up the transport, he wondered how much this jaunt would cost, not that money was an issue. The cabin appeared capable of holding them all. The seats sported an undistinguished brown vinyl, hard but serviceable. The backs of the seats were designed to allow a line of sight around the whole cabin. *All the better to spot the carnivore planning to eat you.*

Jose heard the cabin door bang. Turning around, he spotted a ferret-faced skinny dude coming down the aisle, followed by a big man with an enormous beer belly dragging him down.

"Hey, call me Dez. This here is Clyde." Dez gave a two-finger salute from his brow and kept moving, nodding and saying hello.

Clyde stopped at Jose's seat, extending his hand. "Nice to meet you. And you are?"

"Jose. Nice to meet you, Clyde."

"Oh, you must be Miss Preston's brother. You look so much alike." Jose flushed.

"No, her brother is further up. I'm her boyfriend."

Now Clyde flushed. "Sorry. It must be the shades." Nodding amiably, Clyde moved on to introduce himself to the others. Jose overheard him explain to Captain Cobby that they had joined the expedition as extra hands to help wrangle animals at a zoo. *For heaven's sakes, is she still going through with this?*

Jose sat back in his seat and glanced out the window. From out of nowhere, two sets of tiny wizened hands shot out to grab Jose's pants, hauling themselves up to make themselves comfortable on the seat next to him. Two white-faced monkeys had somehow slipped through the door and managed to locate Jose where they decided to seek refuge. Wouldn't he love to watch Senior Brooks' face if he could see this? Yeah, he would watch him in Hell where he belonged. Thanks to Echo, he'd been dispatched by the mysterious creatures which resided in her antlers, melting him down to less than the crud on the bottom of Jose's shoes.

He absently stroked the monkeys that had once played a short, happy act in his childhood. Taking stock, Jose realized his shock over the discovery of who had murdered his parents and the unveiling of Chloe as his kidnapped sister, was finally starting to dissipate. *But where did all this anger come from?* He realized he sounded like a petulant angry child. Jealousy? *Boy, no wonder Abby's distancing herself from me.* Her plate runneth over and his anger, while understandable, was of no help to her. He made a note to himself not to overreact to anything while he was still digesting the brutal events and discoveries at Chloe's—no, not Chloe's—the despicable slime ball, Omar Nasir's, mansion. Chloe had *never* been his daughter.

Making an effort, Jose turned to the elderly monkeys to find solace in their warmth and the distant memories of the joy he had shared with them so long ago in Costa Rica.

You can read more by going to Amazon and clicking on Hive, Species Intervention #6609 Book 4.

To You, My Dear Reader,

I want you all to know how heartfelt my appreciation is that you have taken the time to read my books. Being an author is one of the most torturous professions out there. Many of us live on the thanks of our readers alone. If anyone cares to leave me an honest review on Amazon.com, Goodreads.com, Smashwords.com, Kobo.com or Barnes and Noble, I would be ever so grateful. You can leave a review on Barnes and Noble and Goodreads without having made the purchase there. Some of you are unaware that Amazon, in particular, promotes books based on the amount of reviews a book gets. No reviews . . . the book will stay a secret.

Don't be afraid to make suggestions or criticize the writing. How else is one to improve? Stay tuned for the next book in the Species Intervention Series, *Armageddon Cometh.*

J. K. Accinni

Author's Page

J. K. Accinni was born and raised in Sussex County before moving to Randolph, New Jersey, where she lived with her husband, five dogs and eight rabbits, all rescued, and currently resides in Sarasota, Florida. Mrs. Accinni's passion for wildlife conservation has led her all over the world, including three trips to Africa, where ten years ago she and her husband fell in love with a baby elephant named Wendi, who had been rescued by a wildlife group. That baby is the inspiration for the character Tobi, the elephant featured in her fourth book, *Hive*.

The character of Caesar is inspired by a real life iconic tiger from the Big Cat Habitat and Gulf Coast Sanctuary in Sarasota. A portion of the proceeds from her third book, *Armageddon Cometh*, will be donated to the sanctuary in support of the enormous expense required to house and feed the displaced wildlife in their care. Mrs. Accinni invites her readers to visit bigcathabitat.org to view the astounding facility and plan a visit with your family.

Mrs. Accinni also invites you to visit her webpage at www.SpeciesIntervention.com, where information on the Big Cat Habitat and Gulf Coast Sanctuary can also be viewed. Readers are encouraged to comment about the book or your own creature experiences.

www.ingramcontent.com/pod-product-compliance
Lightning Source LLC
Chambersburg PA
CBHW070016260626
47159CB00005B/1823